ALIEN SAVAGE'S STOLEN BRIDE

BRIDE

JUNO WELLS

CONTENTS

FOREWORD

Alien Protector's Rescued Bride is a stand-alone but is part of the Draconian Warrior's Series.

You'll enjoy it more if you start at the beginning!

Alien Warrior's Captive Bride

MANY THOUSANDS OF YEARS AGO, DEEP IN THE EXION star system, the first Draconian female entered the Cave of Ascension. She passed through the luminous waters, noticing tiny glowing blobs moving about in the water. Whether they were finless fish or worms was difficult to tell, for they had the characteristics of both as well as thin filaments growing out of their frail bodies.

Knowing the Cave must be her divine destiny, the first queen forced herself to submit to the will of the gods. She walked slowly through the bright waters, emerging a queen on the other side. Her people were equal parts awed and terrified when she disappeared beneath the eerie luminescent liquid, for none had dared to pass through the radiant waters before.

Taking her rightful place as the leader of her people, the queen found that all was well for a brief time. Soon her sleep became restless. A suspicion crept forward from the back of her mind, as she felt something strange growing in her body. It moved around and playfully tickled her insides. Since she had no fever nor evidence of disease upon her skin, horns, or wings, the healers assured her that all was well.

Then the nightmares started, and she never knew a moment's peace thereafter. Every day was a struggle to shut out the dark voice growing ever stronger in her mind. Once the symbiont took full control of her faculties, the young woman was forced to stand idly by while the creature wreaked havoc on her people.

From that day to this, every Draconian female has been forced to walk through the Waters of Ascension, thus becoming a queen in her own right. Those who failed to ascend were killed or sold into slavery. Death was preferable, since a Draconian female slave could look forward to a lifetime of torture by beings furious with their treatment at the hands of the Draconian empire.

A millennia slipped idly by, while the evil of the Cave fell into myth. Ascension came to be known as a coming of age ceremony for young females and the Draconians were taught to love this sacred right, thus perpetuating the Age of the Symbiont. The first symbiont was long lived, and few knew it still wandered the verse looking for plunder and warriors.

As the decades flew by, the queens grew discontented, fought among themselves and battled with each other over warriors. They seemed to grow stronger, to crave chaos, and to feed off the misery of others. Little did the Draconians know, but the luminescent creatures floating in the waters of the Cave of Ascension were not some strange anomaly naturally occurring on their planet, but rather the spawn of a soul sucker that had been driven from a nearby world.

Meanwhile on Earth, the environment was deteriorating, turning the oceans into putrid acidic cesspools devoid of all life forms. The lives of many males were lost in an effort to clean up the contamination, and then the worst-case scenario came to pass. A new pathogen emerged and locked onto the male genome. It took time to develop an antigen, costing more lives still. By the time all was said and done, the ratio of males to females was seriously unbalanced —four females to every male.

Just when humans were losing all hope of survival on their harsh world, aliens made contact with the peoples of Earth. They not only offered to help manage the environmental disaster, but also provided much-needed medical supplies and foodstuffs. In return, the aliens requested the one thing Earth had a surplus of.

Voluntary human brides were offered in exchange for the supplies. Many women were happy to relocate to a pristine new planet with an accommodating alien husband. It beat the alternative, which was living in huge crowded bio-domes.

A large group of human brides were stolen by pirates intent on selling them to the highest bidder. Incompetent fools that they were, they strayed into a spatial anomaly and ended up in Draconian space. Just when the brides' situation seemed hopeless, they were rescued by Draconian warriors. The fight that ensued was one of mythical proportions, resulting in the ship and crew escaping back to normal space.

This is the story of those warriors and the human women they rescued settling a new home world under the protection of the Intergalactic Council of Planets. Unfortunately, the parasitic queen escaped as well. Now the Draconians are always looking over their shoulders, searching for the missing parasite. They do all within their power to ensure the creature does not begin propagating among the human population.

1 / DOMINANCE
ARGON

These primitive stonecutting tools feel good in my hands. The weight is balanced nicely, and they're easy to handle. I place the chisel carefully and strike the hammer soundly against it. The resounding metallic thud is music to my pointed ears. While turning the thick metal stake from side to side, I watch the image in my brain grudgingly take form. Once my mind and hands join together as one, there is no stopping me from creating a masterpiece.

My heart is hardened to all else except creating a keep to house me, my hoard, and at some distant point in the future, my family. Some few of us Draconians are of the old blood. We lust for things the others care little about, such as precious metals and gemstones. Most of the other dragon warriors lust for females. Fortunately, more human females flock to our new planet every day, eagerly looking for mates among our people.

My inner dragon's eyes roll right over their slight human forms in favor of admiring the huge metal spirals on the building our people built to house the ever-growing population. Those spirals fascinate me to no end. I stare at them for endless hours, studying the sensual curve of the metal and admiring their strength and beauty. My dreams are filled with the way their delicate twists and turns reach for the stars.

Today my hammer sings as I work, and the sound quickens my pulse. I'm obsessed with creating my own sanctuary. One carved of stone with delicate spirals that spread towards the heavens. On the very top will be a platform where I can perch and look out over the vast wild landscape of this pristine new planet. I will be king of my own castle and luxuriate on a hoard of treasure, one deep enough to make me the envy of every other dragon warrior on this planet. They will fly from other continents to get a glimpse my hold. However, none will dare to come close to what is mine. My muscles ripple beneath my scales at the thought of rending them limb from limb for coming too close to my territory.

If they transgress, I will remind them what it means to be a pureblood dragon. I can almost feel my inner dragon clawing to get out, to attack rival males. Unfortunately, our ability to transform was taken from us long ago. It was one of the many features selected out and sent to the scrapheap by those who modified our ancient bloodlines. The one thing they couldn't seem to eradicate is our racial memories. Draconians share a pool of deeply recessed collective memories. Those of the old blood, like me, we remember the feeling of shifting to our true form. The thrill of flying and lighting up the world below with our flames.

My nostrils fill with the smoke of my line. I breathe out of my mouth and suck it back in with my nose. It calms me, allowing me to continue working on my stronghold. Much like our scent, the makeup of our smoke is unique to each line, and each male of the line carries his own unique biological markers. We no longer breathe actual fire, but my smoky breath blows hot enough to catch a combustible item on fire.

I am rankled by the unfairness my clade has endured at the hands of our brethren and the new human queens. It causes my anger to rise hard and fast, igniting like matches. They see us as primitive. They fear our volatility. Therefore, the human queens exiled us far from the city center. They would be well satisfied if we never crossed their line of sight again. Our kind was moved from the bowels of huge battleships to the most remote places on this planet with very little thought to our needs.

Exiled I may be, but they cannot stop me from peering at their glorious new city from the dense forest foliage or forbid me from flying over it at will. The males not of ancient blood are mere shadows of their former selves. They would not dare death by facing me in formal combat over anything less than a capital offense. Even then, they would come at me en masse rather than challenge me in single combat. They are weaklings, the lot of them. Truth be told, they should be wary of provoking my ire. To be honest, I admit to enjoying the thought of being fearsome.

Being forced to seek out a safe haven far from the city, my clade chose this mountain to call home. Stone Mountain is composed of nearly solid rock and is good for carving. This mountain will house my entire clade, each of us carving out a spacious suite for our family unit. I choose to carve intricate flora and fauna into my walls. It represents my love of nature and the hunt. Each of my family will carve whatever is dearest to his heart into his personal space.

As the oldest and strongest, I claimed the highest vantage point for myself. Glancing over my shoulder, I look out over a stunning mountain range, filled with slowly dying flame-colored foliage. Winter creeps upon us, so I double down on my effort to carve a home from this magnificent stone. It responds so well to my tools, allowing intricate vines, floral designs and whatnot to come to life. Each detail is rendered according to my own imaginings.

Some would consider this an inglorious task compared to thrill of battle, but I do not think so. Creating order from chaos calls to my very soul, for I am born of a long line of craftsmen. Before coming to this sector of space, our need to create had to come secondary to fighting our queen's many wars for riches and territory. This is no longer the case. Now we are free to do our own bidding.

Our mountain will become a monument to all that is Dragon. Even now, the hammers of my spawn-mates sing in unison with my own. Knowing we are each creating a unique thing of beauty fills my soul with peace. One day our young will fly around, playing together, and we will take turns teaching them the old ways. In order for that dream to come true, we will have to mate.

At least on this new home world, we no longer obligated to serve a vicious Draconian queen. Human queens are docile by comparison. More importantly, they care little for the goings-on of my clade. They have sent us away and forgotten us.

The five of us have stuck together through thick and thin, four scion always flocking around our sire. He insists upon taking up a lower position overlooking a large body of water. Where I love the forest, my sire's heart covets all things damp and moist. Images flit through my mind of him flying low over the lake, dipping one wing at a time into the cool refreshing waters. He enjoys fishing and keeping ornamental water plants and small, colorful nonedible aquatics. All the males of our clade have different interests, yet we fit seamlessly together. It is how a family should be.

The corners of my mouth turn up slightly. Few males are fortunate enough to find a breeding partner, much less ensure all four of his eggs were safely hatched. My sire did this and managed to keep us all close as well. If and when my days of breeding come upon me, I can only pray to be as successful as my sire.

An irritated voice disrupts my internal thoughts. "Do you not hear the trumpet, Argon? It is time to eat, and I have never known you to miss a meal."

I drop my tools and spin to face off with my youngest and most foolish spawn-mate. Without conscious thought, my wings flare out and I hiss at him. I do not like other males in my personal space, even ones related by blood. His eyes should not be looking upon what is mine. Slowly, I realize his eyes are not wandering, but remaining fixed on me. It takes a moment for my blood to cool.

Meanwhile, Narcis stands in the doorway, blocking out part of the sunlight with his bulky form. His green scales are much like my own and glitter in the sunlight. His hands are fisted at his side, with his primary claw extended as if he expects a physical confrontation from me.

A dark thrill snakes up my spine as I realize he sees me as dangerous. He should, but I would never attack my own blood. I frown, realizing that's not quite true. If he came into my space, I'd give him a few bruises to remind him not to transgress in such a way again. Stepping in front of the large crate containing my hoard, I imagine pulling off every finger that touches my personal effects.

Shaking off feelings of violence almost immediately, my voice comes out harsh and deep. "Do not dare to set one foot into my keep, Narcis. You will not like how I defend my territory."

He looks almost hopeful for a moment. "Perhaps you can make my face look like yours."

All my anger evaporates in the space of a heartbeat. My wings relax and I grin at his handsome and hopeful face. "Do not rely upon me to give you battle marks. You must earn them in a glorious mêlée like the rest of us."

His wings drop, barely touching the rocky outcropping behind him. "The battles are few and far between since coming to this world. You know this, Argon."

Padding forward, I reach out and push him back off the cliff playfully with one hand. "Stop dragging your wings like a hatchling." We both laughingly tumble off the precipice and take to the air, gliding safely to the ground. We have played this way since we were small hatchlings, and such irreverent behavior no longer becomes a full-grown warrior. Yet, no one is looking, so we persist.

I tease him with good suggestions for getting mauled. "You could be gored by a wild beast on a hunt. The huge meat-eaters are brutal on this world."

His eyes light up. "I have been thinking of killing one to make a rug for my new domicile."

I chuckle at his turn of a phrase. Domicile is a word he got from the humans. Dragons have aviaries, holds, keeps, strongholds and territory. Domicile is a weak word used by inferior beings and strong evidence that he spends too much time in their company.

Narcis is barely out of his adolescent phase. He was the last egg my father hatched. We all watched and waited to see if he would be strong enough to break out of his shell, and we celebrated when the fledgling showed his strength and will to live. His hatching party was the first time I drank ale. Fond memories flood my mind, and I decide to assist my spawn-mate in obtaining battle scars.

"I will hunt with you on the morrow. Do not expect me to save you from getting wounded. Your simple face could use some decoration."

He grins, slapping one bare shoulder with his hand. "If not my face, my arms or shoulders would wear marks proudly as well." Ever the optimist, that's my spawn-mate.

Since we usually wear only trousers made of tanned animal skin, his secondary choice locations for battle marks make sense. Looking down, I admire my many scars, and my chest puffs up with pride. Though the human queens might turn their faces away, I know my proud strong body is not something to be ashamed of. It is their loss for not seeing my worth.

REBECCA

I SIT IN THE DRACONIAN VERSION OF A LEARNING center trying to absorb all the information I can on their people and culture. We spent a lot of time with them on the voyage here, but most of were so traumatized by our mad scramble to survive on Earth and make our way off world, we self-isolated a lot. I slept, cried, and just tried to convince myself to put it all behind me.

These pods are kind of cool. I keep looking for some way to organize the supposedly self-paced learning modules. So far, I'm getting that their DNA was mixed with that of dragons thousands of years ago. No, I skim the material again. The dragon DNA was mixed with humanoid DNA. That's not exactly the same thing. Looking more closely, I discover their species had it both ways. Some are humanoid mixed with dragon DNA and others are dragons mixed with humanoid DNA. I guess that explains why some of them are smaller and look more human than others. Why does this have to be so complicated?

I push the button for more information and a hot beverage in a cup comes sliding out of the huge computer in front of me. Oh, that's nice. Taking a sip I realize that either I don't know how to use the machine or it's scanning my life signs and gave me this nice relaxing drink because I was getting frustrated. Strangely enough, I'm good with either option. Honestly, it's not the strangest thing to happen to me since I've been sheltering with the Draconians.

This huge room is full of these enclosed learning pods. They're small, but once you learn how to operate the machine, it allows you learn at your own pace and skip around to zero in on what interests you most. I honestly thought I was doing pretty well until it spit this drink out at me.

Sipping the beverage, I prompt it to show a full biological scan of a Draconian male. I always turn away when they walk past. At first it was because I didn't want to stare and be considered impolite or make them feel uncomfortable in any way. After I discovered they don't care about those things, I did it because I was too afraid and embarrassed to talk to them.

A full-size three-dimensional representation of one of their males appears right beside me. And he's buck naked. Shocked, I glance around and find several other clear pods have the same 3D image showing. The other women are smiling and more curious than embarrassed, so I try to act chill as well. Yeah, I'm standing here with my drink, just analyzing this naked alien like this situation is totally normal.

The image solidifies to the point that he looks like a real person, and it startles *me* to the point that I almost spill my drink. *Way to go, Rebecca Ann. You're so not cool.* If I could get rid of that critical voice in the back of my mind, I'd probably turn out into a mature, articulate adult woman instead of a sniveling coward.

I jump again when the image begins pointing out his body parts, starting at the top. Truth be told, this lesson is kind of fascinating. Most of the males here don't have hair. Although they range in color from green, brown and blue to purple and deep teal, their skin has scales with a bit of pattern to them. I've already noticed that they're all totally ripped, with muscles sitting on top of muscles. It's sometimes difficult not to stare. I learned rather quickly that the warriors love to be noticed. Since staring indicates a possible interest, they'll approach you with gifts and ask to spend time getting to know you if you stare at all.

I'm fascinated by their wings. They are huge, and not all of them look alike. Some look like bat wings and others are something a little smaller and more elegant. Draconians also have pliable horns that move back when they're embarrassed or being submissive. Most of them have dinosaur-like tails and a few even have little round or heart shaped bulbs on the tip. Most have dark eyes that are almost black. A few have green or purple eyes though. I even saw one with orange eyes, but he had orange scales to match. That guy was super gorgeous and had about ten women following him around everywhere he went. I suppose he's what you call spoiled for choice.

When the training image gets to his dick, I blush furiously as he lifts it up and shows off all the stunning ridges, rings and bumps. Squeezing my legs together, I try not to imagine how amazing that would feel during sex. They've clearly made him jumbo sized so we can better see all the details, cause no man has a dick that big. He has a big bump with a soft pliable ridge sitting on right top of it. He's talking about how it's designed to stimulate a female's something or another. The translator they implanted doesn't always have a human word for every Draconian word. Sometimes it just sends mental images like it's doing now. I'm getting a visual of a female Draconian's privates, and there is a horseshoe-shaped ring his bulge is meant to bump against. Human women are clearly made differently from Draconian women, but having that stimulating my clit during sex would probably feel awesome.

When my clit starts to throb, I slam my hand into the button to shut down the machine. I've got to get outta here. Flinging the sliding door open, I make a run for it. My face flames when several of the women notice and laugh at me. At least they weren't pointing and laughing, so it could have been worse, I suppose. This is another of my strange idiosyncrasies, trying to find the silver lining in every horrible situation.

There is a data pad with information loaded into it tucked away safely in my bag. I just need to find a quiet spot and read up on this subject the old-fashioned way. Yeah, that sounds like a good plan. It will be much less embarrassing than interacting with a naked fake Draconian dude in glass pod where everyone can see. Images of his body flash through my mind. Truth be told, I wouldn't have wanted to miss the 3D visual. If a picture is worth a thousand words, that training program is worth a thousand pictures in my humble opinion.

Once I exit the building, I meander around looking for a good spot to relax. They've given us rooms in a posh holding facility, but I don't want to be stuck indoors on such a nice day. I've noticed the weather getting nippy, and I suspect winter is coming soon. Therefore, I intend to spend time outdoors while I can.

Outside the building they built to house the unmated females, there is a garden with a fountain, seating, and an assortment of strange alien flowers. I've already been assured the huge moving flowers are not carnivorous. Yeah, I actually asked that, and the response I got led me to believe the warrior thought I was a little on the simple side. He kept the explication short and used small words. It was all kinds of embarrassing. The thing is, that experience didn't even break my top ten most embarrassing moments in life.

I find a quiet spot and snuggle in for a read. Though the breeze is turning nippy, it's still nice to be outdoors. I'm vaguely aware that people are coming and going, mostly women. I've been with the Draconians long enough that I'm on high alert all the time. I slowly relax into the moment and just enjoying being on this beautiful world.

My sire's deep voice says, "Better late than never. Take your places, my scion."

Narcis and I both jog over to the mouth of the cave that spans a cavernous space we use for a great room. It is spacious and composed of three levels inside of the mountain home we now share. The half-carved family table is a reminder that our surroundings are a work in progress at the moment.

We sit quietly as our sire prepares to speak. His scales are taking on the shiny silver edging associated with age. Our elder's quick dark eyes are always alert, proving he misses nothing going on around him. Lifting his wings, he begins to speak. His words remind me why he is considered one of the greatest orators of our time.

"Before we take nourishment this day, I wish to speak to you regarding the next step in our plan to settle this world." Looking from one to another of us, his expression turns tender. "I have fought endless battles for the right to mate and to keep each of you safe. My reward has been watching my spawn grow into strong and capable warriors. When I look into your eyes, I see our ancient line stretching forward into the future."

Shifting uncomfortably in my seat, I now know why he has put on his best robe and is standing at the podium that contains the written record of our line. The old man's train of thought makes a certain kind of sense. We are no longer ruled by Draconian queens and have been granted freedom by our new human queens. This is the first time in our family's history that we are on a safe planet with breed-compatible females. It stands to reason that he wishes us to take mates to ensure our line continues.

The problem is I have absolutely no desire to be bonded to a human queen. They are weak and talk over each other in high-pitched voices. My primary annoyance with them in general is they never seem to shut up. In short, they're too irritating to keep about. Just thinking about it makes a vein in my forehead throb.

That doesn't keep my sire from continuing his sermonizing. "I command that each of my spawn begin to socialize among the human females. I am confident you will be selected by worthy queens. Once our keep is complete, the queens will be brought to your personal spaces, and you will allow them to breed you. Within a turn of the seasons, our clade will be blessed with many young." As if sensing some reluctance on our part, he adds with quiet dignity, "I will see my line continue before I take my last flight into the dark abyss."

I can't help the snort that escapes my mouth at his lofty words. When his dark eyes turn on me, I refuse to squirm like a hatchling. Instead I tuck my wings tighter behind me in a show of respect and speak my piece. "You will live to see my spawn's spawn have young. Do not speak about taking your final flight like it is a pending concern."

"Much like your distinguished sire, you have strength of character, Argon. That is a quality to be respected in a warrior. However, one fact remains." Naturally, he takes a dramatic pause before continuing. "Until I draw my last breath, I lead this clade. Therefore, I will speak, and you will do my bidding."

Properly chastised, my wings droop ever so slightly. I chafe against being commanded to mate, but I will hold my tongue this day. When my sire's eyes drift to the others, he finds only submissive scion apparently delighted to do his bidding when it comes to human queens.

He steps back from the podium, and I can almost see the gears turning in his brain. Closing the distance between his favorite oration spot and the table, he drops down into the largest chair. Gesturing at the table, he speaks calmly. "Eat. We will nourish our minds while we nourish our bodies." The old male is not fooling anyone. Now that he has made his demands, he will smooth things over with humor and gentle guidance. I well know his ways and they will not work on me.

Glancing down the table at the feast set out before us makes my mouth water. My mind forgets about any petty grievance over being forced to breed in favor of eyeing the huge slabs of meat placed down the center of the long table-top. Everything looks and smells delicious. There is foul and fish and red meat aplenty. Indeed, we are now spoiled for choice.

On this lush new world, game is abundant, as is gemstone and precious metals. Such bounty has been unknown to my clade. While serving on Draconian vessels in the before times we ate only nutrient-dense bars of pressed protein. I am continually grateful to be on this world rather than under the rule of Draconian queens.

My spawn-mate's prong comes out to spear the huge chunk of meat situated between us. My knife is drawn and covering his eating utensil before he can take it away. I growl a warning deep and low in my throat before snatching the huge piece of meat onto my plate. It's dripping blood, and so huge my plate cannot be seen around the edges of the generous chunk. Something dark and dangerous snakes through my gut. I'm so thrilled that I can hardly keep the feral grin off my face. I won and the meat is mine. That's all that matters.

Valixon frowns at me in a highly disapproving manner. "Why are you such a barbarian?"

Stabbing the meat with my knife to stabilize it, I slice off a chunk with my claw and toss it into my mouth. My tail twitches with excitement at the taste of juicy blood. Swallowing my first victory bite I preen a bit. "We can't all be poets, Val. Some of us live for the fight." I should not insult my brother's favorite hobby, but the words are out of my mouth before I consider if this is the proper time and place for such teasing.

Taking a smaller piece of meat from a nearby platter, he eyes me with disdain. "Yes. The fight ... for food in this perfectly civilized environment must fuel your baser instincts in some way."

When he puts it that way, my behavior does seem a bit petty. Instead of apologizing for being overly competitive, I slice off a piece of the meat that I won and toss it to him. When he catches it with his prong, I quip shamelessly. "Everything is a competition to apex alphas. That you are still surprised by my need to dominate speaks to your intelligence—or lack thereof."

Shaking his head, he grumbles. "Only one such as you

could derive gratification from fighting over a big bloody slab of meat with your own spawn-mate."

"I gave you a consolation prize. Stop feeling bitter and get used to me being dominant. One day I will be standing at that podium, and you will be required to follow my orders."

It is apparently my spawn-mate's turn to snort a laugh. "In order to lead, you must prove yourself by successfully spawning young of your own. My experience mingling with the human females leads me to believe they would not elect to share their beds with a male such as you."

I stop cutting my meat to glare at him. "What exactly is a male such as me?"

"A male with rough manners and little concern for others." Taking a bite of the meat I tossed him, he regards me pensively before shoving the whole piece in his mouth. I try to concentrate on eating again as I process his words. Is this how he sees me? I cannot believe that is true.

He sounds off yet again. "Perhaps it will be you who ends up following my decrees in the end, Argon."

I nearly choke on piece of meat as I swallow. The thought of kowtowing to Valixon makes my chest hurt, not to mention my ego. If I carve my keep into this mountain, it will become a deeply ingrained part of my soul. Leaving it would break my spirit. Living here under Valixon's rule would also infuriate me beyond measure. Before I can fly across the table and beat that thought from his mind, my father interrupts our conversation.

"You do us proud by moving among the human queens, my scion. Now that they have some familiarity with you as a male, you are properly poised to engage in mating rituals. Have any shown an interest in selecting you?"

Suddenly, Valixon's head dips and his demeanor

changes. I slow my eating in favor of hearing his response. "I have my sights set on a particular female. She has hair the color of fire, and her scent calls to me. Unfortunately, she does not see me among the many."

I freeze with a piece of meat halfway to my mouth as I try to imagine my mild-mannered brother mating a human queen. It all quickly clicks into place in my mind. He is weak. Human queens are even weaker. Perhaps it would be a match. I glance over at the podium and a wave of anxiety washes over my body at the thought of my brother mating before me.

Totally unaware of my panic, our sire attempts to give Valixon some sage advice. "It is good that you have narrowed your selection. Perhaps you should begin sharing your hoard with this queen you covet."

It's a bold and unexpected suggestion. Naturally, Valixon is shocked at our sire's words, as are the rest of us. Val chokes on a bite of food and slams his fist into his chest repeatedly in an attempt to dislodge it. No one thinks to render assistance, because it is a well-known fact that our kind has one genuine flaw. Our throats are narrower than is advisable for eating. We are taught to chew well early in life. As a general rule, males that can't properly feed themselves don't deserve to live. Therefore, we all stare and wait to see if he will survive.

I'm fascinated when his dark green scales begin to turn black and his wings flare out dramatically. That happens when we don't get enough oxygen. A full-blown choking episode is a sight one doesn't see very often, especially in a full-grown warrior. We're all riveted on his attempts to extricate the bit that's keeping him from drawing a clean breath.

Narcis begins counting off the microns it takes Val to

succeed. I grin at my youngest spawn-mate. Counting is a good call because it increases the excitement of the moment. Will he live or die? I certainly hope he lives but if he doesn't, perhaps I can lay claim to his hoard. I'm only half joking with myself about that thought. He isn't going to die, is he?

Finally, a bit of meat comes flying out of his mouth and lands on the table. My poor spawn-mate clings to the edges of the table and gasps for air. His scales slowly lose their dark edges, turning green once more.

Before anyone can speak, I reach out, grab the piece of meat with the tip of my knife and pop it into my mouth. A tiny evil part of my soul is delighted when my entire family gapes at me in shock. Doing things that others would not dare makes me dominant. Shocking them isn't nearly enough so I smack my lips together as I chew and announce. "Tastes like death."

Val shakes his head despondently. "I can't believe you did that."

I find myself preening again. "Of course not. That's why I'm going to be the one standing at that podium one day instead of you." Pointing to my head, I state proudly. "My brain never rests. I'm always thinking about ways to get ahead, increase my hoard and demonstrate dominance. I run probability scenarios in my head to ensure the success of the quantity of decisions I make each day." Pointing my knife at each of my spawn-mates, I continue. "It's an unfortunate fact that I can think circles around the lot of you. Since I also dare behaviors no other being would, that makes me superior in all ways."

I may have gone too far this time, because no one speaks, not even my sire. They all just sit there mirroring the same stunned expression. I lift my chin and continue digging myself deeper into the hole I've apparently chosen to embarrass myself to death in. "When my hold is finished, I plan to simply fly over the city and chose my own queen." Pointing my knife at Valixon, who is still gasping slightly, I continue my shameless outburst. "I refuse to bow and scrape before a queen, hoping to find favor with her. Instead I will pick the largest, plumpest, and most desirable female out of the lot of them all and carry her away in my claws. She will be grateful to be my queen, because I am a born leader."

Now, I know warriors don't select queens, so I don't even know where this idea came from. I suppose I'm hoping my thoughtless spewed words will drive home what a despicable person I am, so my sire doesn't press us into mating right away. Between Val almost choking himself to death, and my brazen rant, I must admit that we are not presenting as very capable males this day.

My sire sits his metal drinking cup down on the table and folds his hands in his lap. He takes a moment to look directly up into the air for a precious few moments before speaking. If I'm at all dramatic, it surely must be a personality trait I inherited from him. When his eyes land on me, I find myself eager to see if my ploy worked. His next words demonstrate that I should not have been quite so hopeful.

His tone is both calm and dismissive. "I am not entirely certain where I went wrong with you, Argon, but I intend to figure it out before you are permitted to approach a queen."

Happiness zings through my chest when it becomes clear he will not force me to breed after all. My joy turns sour at his next words. "I hereby forbid you, under penalty of death, from selecting a human queen. You are not to approach one until your spawn-mates have all been selected by their queens. You will pay close attention to the manner in which they lure their queens, and when I am convinced you thoroughly understand proper mating customs, you will approach eligible queens with me at your side."

Narcis snickers under his breath, but my acute hearing does not miss his laugh or the collective gasps of the others. This is a humiliation I do not deserve for my playfully wicked ways. Being punished for my nature rankles me.

Coming to my feet, I unfurl my wings in a breathtaking show of dominance against my own sire. Now that I understand something important is being denied to me, my fury rises hard and fast. "I am the strongest and should be given priority in all things, most especially in mating rights. What if I they end up with the queen that was destined for me?" I barely get the words out through my nearly locked jaw.

Rather than moving back out of the way, my sire rises to his feet. The look on his face communicates he's in no mood to deal with my outburst. I have little sympathy for his predicament, since he's the one who fanned my flame into a full-blown inferno. Instead of arguing with me, he merely points to the ground. "Submit," he snarls. "Do it now, before I lose all patience with you this day."

This is why I hate being second. Alphas abhor submitting to another. Truth be told, it's the reason I have no wish to be selected by a queen. Having a queen means I will be forced to do her bidding in all things. I would have to cater to her every wish, shower her with pretty things and put all my own needs last. What kind of male would want that? It would take all the joy out of living.

Suddenly, I'm questioning why I'm upset about not being first to mate when I really don't even want to be last. My father will live to see us all mated and with spawn of our own. I force myself to calm down, for there is no rush.

A deep growl comes from my sire, alerting me that he's

about to initiate a full-blown physical confrontation with me. Though deep down inside I'm certain that I would win such a confrontation, I bend my knee and lower myself down. Kneeling before my own sire should not pain me this much. I'm being a piece of animal scat, and I know it, so I lower my head and tuck my wings.

He releases an exasperated breath. "You act like a male half your age. Yet, I must force myself to believe that one day you will come into your own, Argon. On that day you will realize that being a leader is about putting the needs of others first rather than compulsively doing absurdly unpredictable things to prove yourself. I truly hope to live long enough to see you become the warrior I know you can be."

"Yes, sire. I apologize for..." It takes me a moment to choose my words because I'm truly not sorry for anything I've done. Deciding to finish with a bit of wit, I look up to catch his eye. "I apologize for stealing my spawn-mate's tasty regurgitated food particle."

Rather than responding with amusement like I'd hoped, his brow creases even deeper. "You were not raised by wild animals, my scion. You may think your antics are born of humor, but I wish you knew that you shamed yourself this day and in doing so, you shamed me as well."

My head drops and I feel my horns slick back against my head. I hate being such a disappointment when all I really want is to have his respect. Perhaps I have misunderstood my role in this family unit.

Without another word, my father stalks off in the direction of his own quarters. Leaving me on my knees communicates his disdain for my behavior. It's the most disrespectful parting he could have made.

Rruk's deep voice sounds off. "Rise and finish your food, Argon. Let us salvage something from this ridiculous day."

Coming gracefully to my feet, I stop short when I see my three spawn-mates all staring at me. They pity me. I can see it clearly stamped on their faces. It riles up my anger again. I do not deserve their pity. Rather than sitting with them, I spin on my heel and grab my bow from the rack near the mouth of the cave.

Without looking back, I head out to hunt. I don't need their tasty food, their crass judgment or their pity. I can get my own meat and sear it to perfection over an open camp-fire. Am I the only male who likes my own company better than that of others?

When the sunshine hits my face, I decide not to go back all day. When I do return, it will be with precious items for my hoard in tow. My hoard will become the biggest and most impressive in all my clade. Also, there will be no queen I must bow and scrape to, taking up space in my hold or stinking up my bed. No, there will just be me. Images of me all warm, comfortable and wallowing in luxuries float through my mind. It is the most pleasant thought I've had all day.

ANOTHER DAY, ANOTHER EMBARRASSMENT. THIS ONE IS about receiving gifts from one of the clans, or clades as they call themselves. Their leader cajoled me into a lunch date and all five of them showed up. They say it is just for friendship, but now they're plying me with gifts. First it was a box of sweets left at my door. Now it's a beautiful braided necklace. It could only be worse if it was a fancy one with jewels. I told them early on no expensive gifts, and they've managed to control themselves.

"It is woven with the symbol of Entares, the Draconian goddess of beauty and joy."

I take the lovely necklace from him and see that it has my name also woven into it. They even spelled it correctly. "Aww, this is really sweet of you, but I can't accept it." I try to give it back.

"We wish you to have it, regardless of if you select any of us for mating."

"I wouldn't feel right."

Pressing it back into my hands, Aldar asks, "Do you

mind if we ask why you refuse to give us a chance? Do we not please you?"

"I think you're all really nice men, but I'm not interested in a clan. You have all been together since you were young. You should stay together. I know you'll find someone looking for a good clan."

Aldar nods, "You have been a reluctant potential queen. It is my hope that you will be a more enthusiastic friend. Perhaps when you find your male and we find our queen, we can still be friends."

My heart squeezes. "You guys really are the best. If you don't find what you're looking for, volunteer for the next trade mission to Earth, and I'll bet you come back with your perfect match in a queen."

A slow smile lights up his handsome face. "We may follow your good advice regarding seeking a queen on Earth. My heart tells me that might be our best course of action. Please keep the necklace as a token of our friendship."

I slip it around my neck even as I fight back the tears. "A girl can never have too many friends. Thank you for being so kind and respectful about this situation."

His hand closes over mine and his smile is bright enough to light up the darkest recesses of a woman's heart. "Spending time with you has been one of the great pleasures of our life. If you ever have need of us, just message us. If we are on this world, we will come to your aid. We will leave you to your reading, Queen Becca."

I give them each a hug and scurry away while my eyes are still reasonably dry. Before I can figure out a quiet place to read, Willow taps me on the shoulder out of nowhere, practically scaring the bejesus out of me. When I jump away, she points and laughs like a fifth grader.

"You shouldn't be such a scaredy cat. The aliens here are really nice."

Willow is barely of age to sign up for transport to the Draconian home world. Unlike most of us, she's not afraid of anything.

Grasping the strap of my messenger-style bag, I respond breathlessly. "I'm still scared from living on the streets back on Earth."

She's standing proud with her long red hair flowing down around her shoulders. The sunlight reflects off her highlights, and she's attracting a lot of notice. I pull out one of my hair clasps and hand it to her. "Tie your hair back, unless you want to draw a crowd again."

She snatches it out of my hand quick as a wink and begins finger combing her hair back. "Thanks, I keep forgetting about pulling my hair back."

Red hair is something we have in common. Where hers is almost fire engine red, mine is more coppery. The locals are fascinated with red-haired women. Willow and I look nothing alike. She's pale as the moon with green eyes and freckles. I have a creamier complexion and hazel eyes that look almost grey at times.

We're both a little on the pudgy side, though I have a few pounds on her. It's something in the food they serve us. At first, I worried that they were trying to fatten us up, maybe with the intention of making a meal of us. I've since come to understand that the men here have all heard about how we were starving on Earth, and they're trying to make it up to us with tempting treats. Let's just say their treats are more than tempting.

Pain lances through my chest when I think of Earth. None of my kin survived the fall, not that I had that many to begin with. I almost didn't make it out myself. The atmosphere deteriorated to the point that we couldn't leave the bio-domes without wearing a respirator. I somehow made it to a Draconian vessel and asked for sanctuary. They were really good to us during the voyage and kept their word about bringing us to a beautiful new home world without forcing us to take husbands right away.

"What are you thinking about? You look a million miles away mentally."

My head snaps up to look into Willow's pretty green eyes. Huffing out an exasperated breath, I come clean with my only friend. "I was thinking about Earth. I'm really glad to have some time to transition. Everything about being here feels strange to me." Glancing around, I see no less than ten Draconian warriors watching us. They're trying to be casual about it, but I hate being stared at. If I could somehow become invisible for a few months, I would.

Glancing behind her, she catches sight of them as well. "Yeah, I never do get used to being observed constantly. I hate the hunger in their eyes. It's too bad women are still so scarce around these parts." Grabbing my hand, she begins pulling me down a path. "I know what you need, and I've got the perfect getaway spot."

Trying not to fall as she pulls me along, I remind her of the rules. "We're not supposed to leave the footpaths." Peering around, I try to make sure there are no ferocious animals lurking. I have no desire to end up being some creature's next meal. They say once an animal gets a taste for human blood, that will become his preferred meat forever thereafter. I swallow thickly, thinking that avoiding that kind of ugly death could be considered a community service in a way, with as many humans as are running around this place.

The next thing I know, Willow is pushing me face first

into a large alien tree trunk. It's likely a tree because of its shape and size. The blue bark is squishy and gives under my nails. She begins shoving my rump, and I understand she wants me to climb. I don't ask why she's not using her words like a normal person. It could be that there are predators around, and we need to quickly get to higher ground. That thought lights a fire under me, and I claw my way up to the first branch and keep moving, to make room for my young friend.

The moment she's on the branch with me, she pulls away a thick vine and wraps it down one arm ending at the wrist. She grabs the end in her fist and falls back off the branch. I jerk forward, reaching for her, but she's gone before I can get a grip on her. Squatting on the thick branch, I watch her body fall in a graceful downward arc about a hundred paces to the next tree. She grabs onto a branch with her free hand, landing gracefully on a branch.

I know she wants me to follow, but I just can't make myself do something so risky. I sit wrapping my legs around one branch. Holding on with two hands, I watch her swing from tree to tree with the kind of effortless grace I could never hope to match. Suddenly, I'm grinning at her shenanigans. She's so young, happy, and having the kind of carefree play that wasn't possible on a dying world like Earth. My heart thumps with joy at seeing the exhilarated look on her face. Tears sting my eyes as it finally hits home that I don't need to be in survival mode all the time now.

We've been in the trees for over an hour when I get a call of nature and have to climb back down. After having a bird's eye view of the terrain below for the entire time we've been here, I feel reasonably safe that there aren't any predators about. I slip off into the foliage and begin shrugging out of the full body form suit the aliens wear. Although most of the women wear gowns, it seemed a bit pompous to Willa and me, so we opted for more normal clothing.

Willow swings near, and I can hear her talking. Just when I'm about to answer her, it becomes apparent that she's talking to one of the warriors. She's asking his name, but I can't make out his deeper voice very well. That happens sometimes when my translator malfunctions. I flick the spot behind my right ear where they implanted the tiny device.

Her voice comes again. "Gee, you're really handsome. Your nose almost looks like a snout though, so I don't know how I feel about that."

I cringe at her thoughtless words, hoping she doesn't offend him. I grab some tissues out of my pocket and clean up before spraying my hands with a tiny mister I wear around my neck. I can still hear them talking, but mostly I hear my friend flirting it up with the guy. Shrugging back into my form suit, I head in the direction of the voices. Only when I get there, I don't see anyone.

My feet come to a stop and my ears perk up as I try to listen for them. When no sounds of people talking reach my ears, I scramble up the nearest spongy tree and scout the area visually. In the far distance I see what appears to be a gigantic bird flying away. Birds don't concern me though. When nothing catches my notice, I'm forced to conclude she followed her hot snout-nosed hunk back to the city. She's young and probably got distracted by the guy.

Snorting a laugh, I climb down and head back in the direction of my quarters. If she doesn't message me in a few hours with a tall tale, I'll be very surprised. I sometimes wish I were as outgoing as Willow. Instead I'm cringe-worthily awkward and tongue-tied around men, particularly the really attractive Draconian kind.

Approaching my assigned room, I hurry before the sun sets entirely. I don't know why being out and about after dark is so anxiety provoking for me. Maybe it's because of the bad experiences I had on Earth or because every single thing on this planet is an obvious reminder that I'm on an alien world. Whatever it is, I know it will eventually pass.

Once I'm safely inside my room, I remove the small messenger bag I've kept draped over my torso and grab my data pad. Crashing into bed, I kick off my boots and curl up to read. I like my tiny room. It's cozy and just the right amount of private for my liking.

Something doesn't feel right, but I can't place exactly what it is. Normally, a friend turning up missing would be the thing niggling at the back of my mind. However, I know all the way down to my soul that the males here would never kidnap or harm one of us.

Everything I've seen from day one with these guys leads me to believe they'd sooner cut off their own arm than see a woman harmed. Draconian males automatically defer to women to the point of being absurd. I'd be lying if didn't say it's a little off-putting. They even substitute the word queen for woman, because to their minds, "woman" didn't communicate the correct degree of respect and reverence they hold for the fairer sex.

Since Willow left with the guy she called cute, I'd say there was nothing to worry about. She liked him, and he's Draconian. That means she's safe.

The real problem is everything worries me. I know it's a byproduct of being trapped on a dying world where there was never enough to eat, clean water to drink or a safe place to lay my head at night. Snugging down into my clean comfortable bed, I remind myself that those days are long behind me. We're both safe here, as are all the other women who come here. Crime is practically nonexistent here. I can stop worrying.

After scanning page after page of information on Draconian culture, I begin to get drowsy. But instead of getting up to remove my form suit, I start another educational unit on Draconian procreation. It's so fascinating that I'm engrossed in the material before I know it.

Draconian males can create young through a process called parthenogenesis. It's a fancy word that means their reproductive system is activated by the presence of female pheromones. They incubate eggs in a sack on their hip until they're large enough to be removed to an incubator where they continue to grow.

Dropping the data pad down on my chest, I let that sink in for a moment. I can get pregnant by their sperm, but they can produce children that are practically genetic copies of themselves. I can have male or female children, but they can only make males.

Images flash through my mind of having babies with wings and tiny thrashing tails. The reality of males' breeding should be off-putting, but the thought of having children who are fully Draconian makes me smile. Their eggs are also really cute in a strange way. I want to have a child with my own genes, but the thought of my new husband giving me children as well adds a new dimension to my thinking.

5 / STRANGE GOLDEN DREAMS
ARGON

I'VE HUNTED ALL DAY LONG AND LOADED MY PRIMITIVE sled with four kinds of meat. I strapped the hastily constructed conveyance to a hover board to make it easy to pull along behind my powerful body no matter how much I load it down. Now that the hunting is done, I get to scout for interesting and valuable additions to my hoard. This wild planet is the perfect place to look for artifacts and natural curiosities.

I slip through a spot where two huge boulders butt up against each other, and I have to use my com device to illuminate the interior of a cave. Since I activated a small stasis field around my hovering sled, I don't have worry about wild animals helping themselves to my kills or the meat going bad. My hands run over the surface of the stone walls as I explore.

I suspect this world was once populated by a species that has been long extinct. The reason I believe this is because I have found several hand-made items. Even now my fingers trace over faint lines in the walls that seem more carved than natural. The stone floor beneath my feet also carries a design of sorts.

When I move back through the main cavern, I see a couple of tunnels that shoot off from the central cave. Intrigued, I follow one that winds for some time down a steeper incline. I'm certain that I'm moving deeper underground. The further I go, the dryer the air gets. I pull a tiny respirator from my belt and stick it in my mouth.

When the passageway empties out into a small cluster of caves, I allow my natural inquisitiveness to spur me on once more. The first cave is totally empty. Though the floor is flooded with murky water, I can see the walls carry the same faint design as the main cavern but there are huge cracks running across each wall breaking up the design. Since I don't want to get the filthy water on me, I don't enter that room.

I enter each room, one after another, and discover one is ribboned with a deep red gemstone. I knock a chunk out with the butt of my hunting knife, wishing I had elected to bring a laser pistol. Holding it up to the lantern on my com device, I watch the way it reflects the light. Yes, this stone speaks to my soul. Taking it with me, I step into the last small cave.

This room is sprinkled with a gently glowing amber gemstone. It seems to be bioluminescent. When I touch it, the warmth of my skin melts the surface, leaving behind a sticky residue. I wipe the stickiness off on my pants. I decide it's some kind of mineral. A bit of disappointment settles in my gut that I will not be able to take a sample with me.

Then something interesting catches my eye. It's a raised pool of water with more of the faint indentations covering the sides. Peering down into it, I see it is filled with some kind of gold liquid. Dragons do love gold, so it's impossible for me to refrain from dipping my hand into the cool liquid. The liquid has a relaxing effect on me. I lean against the side of the pool and drag my fingers through the odd fluid, luxuriating in the decadent feel of it moving against my skin.

As soon as I relax into the moment, a strange sensation steals over me. It feels like a multitude of voices whispering to me at the same time. There are millions of questions and wondering statements. *What are you? Why is your blood so hot? You are a unique lifeform. How exciting!*

The strange whispers go on and on for I know not how long. At one point my drowsy eyes see thousands of tiny tendrils the size of a short human hair crawling up my arm. The gold liquid begins spilling out of the pool and moving around the shallow indentations in the walls, creating intricate glowing designs. It's beautiful. Too bad I can't have something like this in my own personal space.

I jerk awake and blink. There is no golden liquid anywhere to be found. Rubbing my eyes, I'm disappointed to discover that it was nothing but a fantastical dream. Coming to my feet, I feel a bit like a youngling deprived of his festival treat. I dust off my pants, grab my red gemstone and begin working my way back through the tunnel to the main cavern. What's worse, I am forced to do it by touch since my com device is no longer functional.

My Draconian ancestors were cave dwellers, so we have fairly good vision in the dark. That makes it not much of an inconvenience. I find that I'm almost cheerful after my short nap. Or perhaps my good mood is because I have found a new and rare gemstone for my hoard and fresh meat for my clade's table.

When I exit the cave, the bright morning sun hits me full force. No wonder I'm feeling so refreshed. I've been sleeping all afternoon and night. I deactivate the stasis around my primitive sled and head back home. Perhaps my father is right about me being impulsive and irresponsible. I must be, to linger in a strange cave napping for so long. Then again, maybe it's my dragon DNA that craves hibernation in such a cool dark place.

I love to hike, and the long trek gives me time to think. Why would I dream about gold that moves? Well, being a dragon means I love precious metals. Perhaps discovering the gemstone triggered some deep-seated greed, making me long for gold. That sounds right, so I let it go.

I've shamed myself before my sire and spawn-mates. Regaining their respect should be my overriding concern right now. My family means well, but sometimes I do not believe they understand me as a person. My competitive nature can get me into trouble. I'm coming to realize that my overreliance on humor to get me out of such predicaments is something that might have served me well earlier in life, but it is no longer acceptable for a male of my age and standing. I hate to go back to beating everyone senseless, but it looks like that's the direction my life is headed. It will cause problems, because that's what happened before I learned to use humor as a buffer.

ARGON

I BLUSTER INTO OUR TERRITORY WITH MY SLED, HAVING prepared a speech of contrition fit to earn me accolades for being mature and responsible. For the first time ever, total chaos reigns in our mountain. If I'd thought for a single moment that my family was still upset with me, I'd have been very much mistaken. Instead they are furious with my spawn-mate, for he has brought a flame-haired, screeching queen into our midst.

She's young, like Narcis, but she has the lungs of a great warrior. She's screaming at him for being rude, selfish and snouty. Since Narcis does have a prominent nose that honestly borders on being a snout, I'm more than amused that she's including it in her litany of complaints against him. I reactivate the hover board under the sled I've rigged so it's sitting on the ground and stand holding my pretty red gemstone as I watch the show.

His fire-haired female is both beautiful and energetic. He's chosen well, for she's plump, speckled with red dots and ripe for breeding. Truth be told, she's a bit young for my taste, and far too angry for my liking, but I'm more than pleased to see her screaming at someone who isn't me. When he tries to disengage, she pursues him out of our great shared space and right outside. When he doesn't stop, she grabs his arm and jerks on him until he does. Then she proceeds to yell at him some more. This is even better than the moving-image shows the humans taught us to love.

Of course, I don't get off without being dressed down by my sire. He hisses, "Wipe that smile off your face. Can't you see that your spawn-mate is in some peril with his new queen?"

Turing curious eyes on my sire, I find that I truly can't wipe the grin off my face. No queen has ever taken note of us at any point in our lifetime. That Narcis has drawn the notice of one so disagreeable seems like a bit of a longshot. She's pushing his chest and yelling for all she's worth. I can help but wonder what her problem is. "Why is she so upset?"

My father responds curtly. "Why do you think?"

Shock rolls through my body. "Did he steal her away from her people?"

"I wish it were something that simple. Listen to her words."

I tune back into their rather loud argument and am rattled by what I hear.

The little queen stands with her hands on her hips, glaring at Narcis. "Well, that was your first mistake. You don't just flirt with a girl, get her all interested and bring her home for your freaking brother!"

"I did not make a flirt with you," Narcis responds incredulously. His horns are standing straight up, his wings are flared out a notch and his tail is curled around his own leg. Truth be told, my youngest spawn-mate is not making a good showing for himself today. He pulls his thumb back to point at his own chest. "You made the flirt with me."

"Yeah, and you never once objected."

"In my own defense, I thought this was a normal inter-action between queens and warriors."

She rolls her eyes and her voice becomes mocking. "No one can possibly be that clueless."

My spawn-mate's wings jerk back in anger and embar-rassment. "Apparently I do lack the clues to decipher human behavior."

Her anger seems to click down a notch. "You can't wander off with a woman and gift her to your brother. You do know that, right?"

"I merely recognized you as the one my brother spoke of and invited you here to make the human flirt with him."

She jabs a finger in his chest as if to drive home her point. Of course her nails are not sharp enough to accom-plish much. He opens his mouth to object once more, but she cuts him off before he can make words. "Not a chance, snouty. Read my lips. I'm not hooking up with your brother."

"Shall I take you back to the city?" Even I can tell by his tone of voice, Narcis doesn't want to take her back. He seems drawn to her. I watch him move closer to her, and I am not certain he realizes the message his body language is sending. Though his mouth says she is for Val, his body says she is for him.

"You brought me here, and now you're stuck with me." The smart little queen, she notices his body language. The clever creature takes a step closer to him, chewing demurely on her bottom lip the way queens are wont to do. After a thoughtful moment, she speaks words fit to rip our family apart. "I chose you, not your brother."

And just like that, our clade has its first queen. Narcis is as stunned as the rest of us. My eyes jump to Valixon. He's perched upon a high ledge on the side of the mountain, watching the spectacle play out below. The expression on his face is one of pure misery. He slowly stands as all faces turn up to stare at him. He leaps into the air and his massive wings unfurl, carrying him towards the forest.

My chest aches for his loss. When my eyes find the offending female, her hands are resting on my spawn-mate's naked chest. Narcis is so uncomfortable that it is painful to watch her attempts to lure him in. It's clear the vixen is ready to mate. If I weren't so angry, I'd be amused that she chose the one member of our clade who has not quite come into his hormones. When he reluctantly turns away, I call out to him, eager to see them momentarily parted.

He comes to me, and the look of conflict on his face reminds me all over again why I hate queens. They are trouble, and always complicate a male's life. Naturally, she can't give him a minute to speak with me. She's at his heels, still talking. "Is this your long-lost brother?"

When my eyes find hers, I know my expression is exasperated. "Long-lost? I've been gone overnight."

Narcis blinks at me, but it is my father's voice that thunders from the side. "You have been gone for three risings of the suns. You were angry. We thought you were pouting and decided to give you space to work out your own problems."

Shock rolls through my body as I try to process his words. It is unbelievable that I have been gone for days.

I quickly recover when the queen speaks to me. "I asked what it is you have there." Everyone is looking at me, and I have a vague recollection of Narcis introducing us while I stood with my mouth gaping open. I'm still focused on the time lapse. Three days? It simply does not seem possible. Instead of explaining why I have been gone so long, I answer the imperious queen's question. "It is gemstone I found for my hoard."

She does the unthinkable by reaching to touch it. Once she touches the precious stone, it's no longer mine-and-only-mine. This young and innocent queen clearly does not realize that we do not touch each other's prized hoard items. I sigh and hold it out for her. "Here. Take the stone and peace be with you."

Allowing me to roll the head sized stone into her arms, she frowns. "I thought this was for your hoard."

My father explains with a level of patience I can't manage at the moment. "Among our people it is considered inappropriate to touch another's prized possessions. Those of us of ancient blood are extremely possessive. We don't allow others in our personal space and if they touch our most prized possessions it makes them less valuable in our minds, and therefore, less ours."

The young queen's mouth turns up into a deliciously mischievous smile. Even as evil as I am, I cannot fathom what she is thinking until she speaks. "Does that mean if I break into Narcis' room and touch all his hoard items that will make them all partially mine?"

Narcis gasps but his astute queen doesn't really need an answer to that question. She shoves the huge gemstone into his arms, breaks away from us, and runs in the direction of my youngest spawn-mate's keep. He bolts after her, but she's light on her feet and got a head start. Unfortunately, Narcis is weighed down by the gemstone and his own bulk. I don't even have to wonder who gets there first, because her laughter and his howls of displeasure echo from the rock walls.

Her behavior is totally unacceptable, and I blame my brethren in the city. If the other warriors didn't spend every minute of every day allowing these females to do anything they wish, my brother's hoard would not be in the process of being violated by this rude human queen.

As if intuiting my thoughts, my sire sounds a warning in my ear. "She is our new queen, and you will respect her in all things."

My head swivels around to look at him. I'm forced to stretch my neck to keep my head from exploding from sheer frustration. "Females are trouble," I grumble.

"It does not matter how much trouble a queen is, they are to be revered. Without a queen, our line will die out. Narcis was selected almost by happenstance. There is no guarantee any of the rest of you will be successful in securing a mate. Therefore, serving and protecting this one is now our clade's highest priority."

"Understood," I mutter grudgingly. Truly, I do understand. Males are required to acquiesce to the wishes of queens. It is the way of our people.

It finally occurs to my sire to ask the one question I do not know the answer to. "Where have you been loitering for three long days?"

Glancing away, I respond quietly. "Visiting with friends?"

"You phrase it as a question, like you do not know where you have been."

My sire's all-seeing eyes miss nothing. It's like his inner dragon can spot deception a parsec away. Huffing out an exasperated breath, I ignore the smoke coming out of my nose and speak the truth. "I explored a cave and came into contact with some kind of toxin that caused me to sleep."

A shake of his head and his expression of disapproval

communicates how adept he thinks I am at screwing things up. I pull my wings up and lift my chin. "At least I didn't stumble into courting rituals with my spawn-mate's preferred queen."

An almost-smile plays about my sire's lips. "Yes. At least you didn't do that. It seems you are not quite as adept as your brother at finding trouble."

"Brother?"

He folds his wings back and draws his hands together in front of his body. It is a pose I have come to recognize as his teaching stance. "We now have a human queen. Therefore, we are obligated to use the humans' preferred terminology for family affiliations."

I can't force myself to keep quiet about this new turn of events. "If they come to our keep, they should accept our preferred terminology."

"Don't be petty, my son."

My lip curls at yet another human term. "I do not like this, not at all."

"Nor do I," my father responds crisply. "It is fortunate that Draconian males are resilient. We've survived by adapting to whatever adversity the 'verse throws at us."

"My brother's queen is to be considered a misfortune? I will make certain I remember this conversation." I emphasize the human term for spawn-mate and the word misfortune, drawing another expression of disapproval from my sire."

"Do not attempt to put words into your sire's mouth, Argon. You aren't nearly clever enough to pull something like that off. Queen Willow is clearly a blessing for our clade. The misfortune was in reference to Valixon for having his heart broken."

I almost cringe at the loud squawking coming from

Narcis' new queen. Surely, we can do something to close her mouth. Fantasies of gagging her, smearing her mouth with engine sealant or taping her mouth shut float through my mind. I realize none of that would be allowed to remedy a queen's noise. Perhaps we can take turns feeding her sweets. This idea has real potential. She cannot screech if she is chewing, right?

The one member of our clade who has not spoken sounds off. "We've survived the rule of vicious Draconian queens. I doubt this small noisy human will destroy our clade." My sire and I turn to Rruk.

"You are correct, my scion. Queens do not react well to change. Once this new queen settles in our midst, all will be well. I am certain of it."

I scratch the back of my neck, growing weary of the drama. "As long as one of us is certain, that is enough for me."

My sire draws himself up to his full height and folds his wings neatly behind him. "I bid you both good day. Mark my words about our new queen. Word had better not reach my ears of you speaking ill of her."

Once he is out of hearing range, Rruk turns to me. "At least he's not leaving you on your knees this time."

I shoot him an annoyed look. "Thanks be to the gods for small mercies."

We both glance in the direction of Narcis' quarters, because now there is laughter drifting to our ears. I wonder how she goes from angry to happy so quickly. It's unsettling and not normal behavior to my mind. Jerking my chin in the direction of our new queen's giggles, I ask wearily "How long has she been here?"

"He brought her here at midmorning. I want her gone."

My head jerks up to look into his eyes. The deep-seated

worry I see there disturbs me. "You can't be serious. Did you not just hear our sire's proclamation on this matter?"

"Indeed I did. Val is grieving the loss of the queen he hoped to one day make his own. Narcis isn't mature enough to mate a queen, and I'm sick and tired of hearing her screaming." Pausing, he frowns. "I like her laughter even less."

"Need I remind you that I am supposed to be the reckless one? What do you suggest we do, steal her away in the night?"

"Just take her back to the city. The males in the city are docile compared to us. They are better equipped to tolerate an annoying queen."

"And if she doesn't want to go? What am to do then?"

Rruk folds his arms over his chest. "She has a friend. Track her down and bring her here to talk sense into this female. She can't choose to mate a male who has not come into his hormones, even if they are age mates."

"Our good sire will lose his mind if we take steps to rid ourselves of the new queen behind his back."

"I no longer care. Would you have Val spend the rest of his life watching his preferred queen in the arms of his own spawn-mate? Queen Willow and Narcis are both too young to know what they want. They would be more playmates than proper mates."

My spawn-mate's clever turn of a phrase does not escape my notice. "When you put it that way, it almost seems like a good deed we're doing." My spawn-mate must think me foolish or weak minded because he doesn't seem to pick on the sarcasm in my voice.

"This queen is too much and Narcis is not yet ready for breeding or the responsibility of maintaining and caring for a queen. You know this, Argon."

"I know that my brother's breeding rights are not to be contested unless by direct challenge. I notice Valixon did not do so. Let us give them some time. Perhaps this queen and Narcis will grow together. If she grows some fondness for him, perhaps he can talk her into being quiet."

"Absolutely not, Argon. All we need is for them to bond. If that happens, we'll be stuck with the little squealer forever."

"That thought makes me no happier than it does you, but such things are not for us to judge. Besides, if you are set on this plan then you can always seek out the friend yourself."

Refusing to look me in the eye, he states quietly. "I find that I am not quite that reckless."

Slapping him hard on the back of the shoulder, I snap. "I was not made to do the bidding of lesser beings. Therefore, do not attempt to trick me into doing the very deeds you shirk yourself."

Rather than listen to him prattle on about this unfortunate situation, I head to my own hold, leaving the fresh meat for him to unpack. I hunt. He cooks and handles food storage. It has always been this way with our clade, each of us being utilized according our strengths and interests.

REBECCA

I TOSS AND TURN ALL NIGHT, WAKING UP EXHAUSTED and sick at my stomach. Okay, I'm a terrible friend and a horrible person. Willow did not come home, nor did she contact me. The next day I discovered her bed hadn't been slept in and her com unit wasn't functional. I call in that favor with clan Aldar, who were kind enough to help me turn the entire city upside down looking for her. After searching every nook and cranny for her and finding nothing, we reported her missing.

We went round and round with every official we could get to listen to us. I'm not entirely certain these guys even understand the concept of crime. They cannot fathom a woman being abducted or being targeted for abuse. They kept insisting that wherever she is, it must be where she wishes to be. If not, they insist the male would have brought her back to her assigned quarters.

Eventually clan Aldar had to leave because they'd accepted an assignment on one of our trade vessels going to Earth. Since then I've been continually scouting the city for her myself. If only I knew she was safe. Images keep running through my mind of her being attacked by a wild animal or falling down a ravine.

It's been ten days. I've cried myself to sleep nearly every night over my failure to act when it might have mattered. Tossing and turning all night, I dream of her being in one desperate situation after another, calling out for the only friend she has. I can't eat, sleep or concentrate for the shame consuming my soul. When push comes to shove, we women are supposed to look out for each other. Only, I didn't.

I roll out of bed on day eleven, spend too long in the shower and get dressed in silence. A few hydration packets and compressed all-weather gear go into my mini-messenger bag before I make my way to the trees where Willow went missing. I've been spending all day there, watching and waiting for her to return. My chest aches and my mind won't be still. I've always been a little worried about life, but now my anxiety is totally off the chain. I'm consumed by the need to find her and know she's okay.

Within a half an hour, I'm perched on exactly the same branch I was the day she was swinging so carefree on the vines. I close my eyes and remember her laughter and how she encouraged me to come to her. I should have done that, but I let my fear and anxiety get in the way. If I had it to do over again, I would join her in a heartbeat and be damned with the consequences.

The wind flutters around me, causing the now-dry leaves to rustle. When I open my eyes, there is a Draconian male about ten yards away. He's just squatting on a thick branch staring at me. The gorgeous man's wearing only leather pants and a utility belt. Most of the ones I've bumped into wear form suits that cover almost every inch of their bodies. His huge green body is the dull green the other warriors call battle drab. It means he's designed for fighting, not breeding.

His dark eyes roam over me, taking in all my curves. It's almost like he's never seen a chubby girl in a tree before. My irritation rises as I imagine him trying to work out how I managed to lift my own body weight high enough to sit so far up. His words startle me.

"You are in the spot where I normally perch to view the city. Move." After staring at me for another second, he adds the word "Please" almost as an afterthought.

Rolling my eyes, I respond without thinking. "How's about no? I was here first, and I don't see your name carved on this branch."

"It's where I sit to admire the spirals on the buildings. You've been here every day for two and half hands of days. Enough. I want you gone from my spot."

Glancing down at his four digits, I surmise he means ten days. "You're right. I've been here for ten long days, and I'll be here every single day until my friend comes back."

His eyes fly open and his wings jerk in a gesture I recognize as surprise. It knocks him off balance, and he almost falls. "You are the screamy one's friend?"

Shock rolls through my body at his carelessly spoken question. Willow has a high-pitched voice that might be seen as screaming. "My friend's name is Willow. She's got red hair. It's much brighter than mine. Is that who you're talking about?"

His expression turns almost disgusted. "Yes. She has red dots that do not wash off."

Suddenly, I find myself moving closer to him. He knows she has freckles. "You said she was screaming. What the hell have you done to make her scream?"

His head tilts. "I do not think you know this female. If you did, you would not ask that question."

What in the name of all that holy is this idiot going on about? "I want to see her with my own eyes and make sure she's not hurt."

His expression morphs into a frown. "Why would she be hurt? Who has harmed her?"

"You, dumbass. Or whoever abducted her. I demand you take me to her right away."

He sighs, managing to look ten kinds of put out. Eventually, he opens his arms to me. "The way is long. You fly with me if you want to see your foolish friend."

"She's not foolish. She's really nice." Without missing a beat, I tack on for good measure. "You, on the other hand, are a bit of an asshat."

As we move closer to each other, he mumbles under his breath. It sounds like he's saying, "This is not something I have never once been told before now."

Great, the handsome brute has been told he's an ass before. Yay me, for recognizing right from the start that he's a bit off. When I get close, he pulls me forward onto the more stable part of the branch and turns me around in his arms. It feels like he's making me the little spoon. I'm not sure how I thought he'd carry me, but this wasn't on my radar. "Are you sure you can fly with me weighing you down?"

His eyes lift to mine and his voice turns soft. "I have always wished to fly with a beautiful plump little queen in my arms. My wings are strong enough for me to fly with a herd beast in my claws. Carrying your slight form will not be unduly taxing."

Shit, the dumb asshat's trying to flirt. Calling me beautiful was a stretch, but he shouldn't have thrown the descriptor plump on as well. I narrow my eyes and respond sternly. "Stop trying to win me over with flattery. I want to be taken to see my friend, and nothing more."

He sighs but nods his understanding. "I do not wish to make you my mate. I was merely attempting to be polite and assuage your fears about my carrying your hefty form such a long distance." From the bland tone of his voice, one might think he was just stating a fact. I can tell from the twitch of his lips that he thinks he's being amusing. Just what I need, an alien with a weird sense of humor when I'm really stressed.

I turn around and reply sternly. "You're not funny. You look as though you should be but you're not." Before he can reply, I turn around, giving him my back.

A snorting wheeze sounds a bit like a laugh. He adjusts his balance and pushes off the branch with both arms around my torso. The minute we begin to climb in altitude, he wraps his legs around mine. At first, I'm too shocked to object. Then I realize he's lifting our bodies into a horizontal position below his flapping wings to streamline our form and cut down on air drag. I need to calm the hell down and let the man fly.

The moment we're in the correct position for flying together, an image of that gigantic bird flying away in the distance on the day Willow disappeared pops into my mind. I know all the way down to my bones that was my friend being carried away by one of these guys.

Barely turning my head, I ask, "Did you take my friend away?"

I get a one-word answer that I'm not sure whether or not I believe. "No."

The word is delivered in a smoky voice that warms the side of my neck. Suddenly, I realize how nice he smells. My hands come up to wrap around his arms, one hand moving back to grasp his shoulder. The moment my hands touch his skin he shifts, lifting his hips slightly back away from my body.

His scales are warmer and softer than I would have imagined. I remember reading that the primitive ones have two forms, a normal one and a battle form. When they're in battle mode, the scales harden to make a virtually impenetrable natural body armor. These men are so alien compared to us that it's not even funny.

I try not to enjoy the closeness of our bodies. This bastard might be lying about Willow, so I can't let down my guard. For all I know, he's torn her limb from limb and eaten her.

I've got to be strong. The minute that thought pops into my head, I realize that I'm already being strong. The old me would have never let a complete stranger that might have abducted my friend take me away like this. Swallowing thickly, I try to frame my behavior as courageous rather than foolhardy and desperate.

We fly for what seems like a long time before I see several mountains in the distance. Mist covers the valleys in between, giving it a picturesque, mystical quality. The visual is like something straight out of a fairytale. Why anyone would leave an area like this to stare at the city is beyond my ability to comprehend.

My body goes rigid when I realize it's probably because the city has women. It slams through my mind that he probably lied about wanting to see the spirals on the tops of the buildings. It wouldn't make sense that every single alien male in that city is staring at red-headed women, but he came to look at the architecture. God, I'm so hopelessly naive. Now they have two of us. I should have gone to the thoroughly unhelpful authorities instead of coming with this man.

His voice is impossibly deep when he whispers in my ear again. "Calm yourself, my plump little queen. We are almost to my clade's hold."

He's called me fat twice now. I think I might actually hate this guy just a bit. If this asshat tries to keep me against my will, I vow to make him regret it in a very serious way. I will gouge out his eyes or something. My real concern right now is Willow. I need to know she's all right.

A short time later, we're circling around the biggest mountain and he careens to the right, bringing us down onto a rocky outcropping near the top. He releases my legs as we alight on the ground, but they feel like limp noodles from being wrapped around his for so long. He bends down and scoops me effortlessly into his arms. After strolling into a cave that's outfitted like a room, he tosses me onto a flat platform that might be a bed.

I can't tell for sure because it has a huge indentation right in the center. Too nosy for my own good, I reach over and smooth my hand over the spot. After a thoughtful moment, I almost burst out laughing when I realize it's shaped like his tail where it meets his back. I glance up at him. Yep, if he were to lie on his back, his tail would fit comfortably in the divot. Searching around the bed, I'm fascinated to discover very slight indentations running horizontally across the top half of the bed. They meet a little above the first indentation. It can only be for one thing, his wings.

His deep voice sounds off from the back of the cave. "My, aren't you a quiet and curious little human."

I find him leaning against a stone bookshelf, or what

will be a bookshelf when he's finished carving it. "Aren't you going to call me fat again?"

Dropping down into what could only be described as a throne chair carved of stone, he smiles. "You are deliciously plump, not fat."

Moving all the way back on the bed to put as much distance between the two of us as possible, I respond tightly. "Human women aren't food. You do know that, don't you?"

He throws back his head and laughs. "I cannot think of any male who would prefer eating a queen over mating her."

I feel my eyes go wide as panic wells in my chest. I bring up both hands, palms out. "We're not mating. You promised me that I could see my friend."

His humor dies away. "I am a male of my word."

"Where is she?"

"Sleeping, I imagine. It's early yet for a queen to be up and about."

"It's midmorning. Why would she still be sleeping?"

Sighing, his expression turns annoyed. "How should I know such things? Human queens are a nuisance, and Queen Willow is more aggravating than most."

Well, we're not food, and he doesn't like humans. For some reason I feel safer. Perhaps that's a mistake, but at least I don't have to worry about him eating me or trying to keep me here to have his babies. Putting up a brave front, I try to put some authority in my voice. "I want to see Willow right now. What have you done to her?"

His expression morphs into one of exasperation. "If she were mine, I would put sealant over her lips and only remove it long enough for her to take sustenance."

He wants to shut her up. That is a huge red flag that something is not right. A man can do a lot of things to shut a woman up, and most of them classify as abuse. Balling my hands into fists, I jump back off the bed and glare at him from across the room. "Look dickhead, I don't care what you think of human women, or of me and Willow in particular. Take me to her, now."

This man is not afraid of me at all. In fact, his face lights up with a mischievous grin. "Aren't you a fierce little queen? Come sit on my lap, and I will soothe you until your friend wakes."

What the hell? My mouth falls open. This guy is all over the place. One minute he hates women, and the next he wants me to sit in his lap. I don't think he know what the hell he wants, and that's kind of concerning. He's just moved from the arrogant prick category to the crazy pants category in my mind.

"Come to me, my plump little queen." His voice has that deep smoky quality again. Somehow, I can smell him from all the way across the room. It hits me hard and fast that he's releasing his mating scent. I've read all about that in the database. It's potent and designed to lure women into their beds. Rumor has it that once you are seduced by one of these guys, you never want to leave again. I'm definitely not hitching my apple cart to this particular piece of crazy.

Lifting my chin, I articulate each word clearly so there's no mistake. "Pay attention to my words. I am not sitting on your damned lap. You need to get the hell outta here until you can control your mating scent, 'cause I'm not interested in smelling it." Okay, that was a blatant lie, but I'm not going to allow myself to fall for some guy I don't know who may or may not have eaten my best friend.

My strong rebuke strikes home. The big sexy freak is out of his throne and stalking towards the mouth of the cave almost before I can scramble out of his way. His tail is whipping back and forth like they do when a dragon warrior is angry or stalking prey. The minute he gets to the edge, he jumps and flies away.

I stand frozen in place, mesmerized by the sight of his powerful wings. My heart is beating wildly in my chest as if trying to escape my rib cage. Even more alarming, my clit is throbbing like it has a heartbeat of its own. What remains of his mating scent wraps around me, luring me back to the place where his scent is the strongest. I refuse to get back in his bed, by sheer strength of will alone.

Instead I turn and begin exploring his personal space. I might be curious to learn more about him, but my priority is trying to find clues about Willow's whereabouts. I shove the image of his muscular scarred chest from my mind and focus on the task at hand. If I find so much as a strand of her hair here, I'll make killing him my life's ambition.

This place looks like it is still in the process of being built. There are stonecutting tools lying about and partially carved reliefs everywhere. I step closer to a gigantic stone desk. It has rolled up papers scattered all over the top. A metal cup holds different kinds of writing implements. Scattered among the papers are flat edged pieces of metal that might be used to draw straight lines and others that are marked which remind me of protractors.

My shaking hands come up to unroll one of the huge pieces of paper. I find a drawing of a building. It's one I've seen before in the city. The building is only a rough sketch but the spiral on top is drawn in amazing detail. Searching through all the papers, I find drawing after drawing of buildings, each with a fancy spiral. I let out a shaky breath when I realize Mister Crazypants truly is an architect. These are professionally rendered, hand-sketched images that appear to be drawn to scale and everything.

He probably wasn't lying about me being in his spot. Something loosens in my chest to discover this bit of information. Perhaps it humanizes him in my mind a bit. It's what I need get ahold of my emotions in this moment. I run my fingers over one drawing, tracing his clean lines. Imagining the huge muscle-bound alien spending hours slaving over these sketches makes me smile. *Never judge a book by its cover* is the saying that most aptly describes this situation.

Moving about his space, I run my hands over everything. Something about the tactile experience of exploring by touch sooths my nerves. This guy has quite a collection of random things. Daggers, gemstones, geodes and knick-knacks of every shape, size, and description decorate the surface of his shelves and tables. It feels like getting a glimpse into a chaotic mind, one that's obsessed with cool spirals and collecting unusual artifacts.

In the far back of the room, there is a glass bubble built into the wall. I touch it too, knowing full well what it is. It's an incubation unit for the eggs he'll produce for some lucky lady one day. My heart softens towards the strange man when I realize he's working so hard to prepare for having a family. He deserves one. They all do.

Just when I'm about to think that everything's fine, I hear Willow screaming. I can't make out what she's saying, but I begin to panic. I run over to the mouth of the cave to look for a way down. Lo and behold, Mister Crazypants drops out of the sky and lands on the stone beside me.

"I will take you down. Talk to your friend. Get her to see that my spawn-mate is not right for her."

My mouth falls open. I'm stunned. All every Draconian male we've met has wanted is to be chosen by us as a mate. But these males apparently don't even want Willow here.

It's a lucky break, in my humble opinion, because who in her right mind would want to stay in the middle of nowhere with slightly unhinged aliens, when there is an entire city full of normal ones willing to move heaven and Earth to make you happy?

I nod my agreement. "I'll do exactly that."

He scoops me up in both arms and glides quickly to the ground with me.

No sooner do I set the lush little queen down than my sire's furious tone trumpets his disapproval. His booming voice carries and bounces off the surrounding rocks, making his threat sound like the thundering of a god. "Under penalty of death, you were forbidden from hunting a queen, Argon."

The plump queen startles at his talk about death and his angry tone. She steps back against me, curling under my arm. The proudest moment of my entire life is slipping my wings around her soft form to ensure she feels protected. Something about this fierce queen cowering pulls out all my protective instincts. My sire is frightening her, and I will not have it.

"Stand back, my sire. Lower your voice and control your anger. I'll not have you terrifying this new queen."

He stops in midstride, gaping at me for a moment before he straightens. It takes him a few moments of hawkishly watching her cling to me to understand he is the cause of her fear. "You have my deepest apologies, little queen. It was not my intention to..."

Before he can finish his thought, Queen Willow comes running out of the common area screaming, "Becca, is that you? Oh my God, I can't believe you came here."

My human queen recovers from her initial shock, shoves my wing aside and steps out to meet her friend queen. I move back to give them space, not fully understanding my suddenly polite and accommodating behavior.

My sire moves to my side, and we watch them walk away together. I've long since realized human queens are not aggressive with each other the way Draconian queens are, but it still seems odd to see them hugging and holding hands as they talk. Their worry slowly ebbs away the more they talk until they are smiling and whispering. When it becomes apparent all is well, my father speaks. Only this time his voice is stern but moderated volume, meaning he does not draw the notice of the human queens.

"Explain yourself this moment, my scion."

Trying to keep the annoyance from my tone, I respond while barely taking my eyes from the humans. "There is nothing to explain. I went to the city to view the spirals, and there she was, sitting in my spot."

His wings jerk as he tries to make sense of my hastily spoken words. When I glance at him, I find him looking at me as though I'm simple. His lips press into a fine line for a moment and then he asks, "You have a special spot you like to sit in to look at the city?"

Huffing out an exasperated breath, I explain as best I can. "I am only interested in the tops of the buildings. My spot is high in a tree. It is the position with the best vantage point to what I most wish to gaze upon." All right, I'm barely making sense, and I know it. Still, I trudge on, because that is how I am. "She's been sitting there day after day for too many days, so I asked her to leave."

His eyes narrow, as if I am lying to him. "That does not explain why you stole her away."

My wings flare in frustration. "Why must you always assume the worst of me? Am I not your scion, like the others who reside here? I did not steal her."

Before I can get worked up, he interjects. "So you say. Did you not say you wished to mate first? Did you not threaten to fly over the city and chose the plumpest and most beautiful queen for your own?" He raises an eyebrow as if to make his point. "And now here she is, wrapped up tight under your wing."

Stretching my neck, I grasp at the last of my control to keep from yelling at my own sire. "I wasn't half-serious when I threatened to do that. Upon speaking to her, I discovered she was nearby when Queen Willow left with Narcis. This new queen, Queen Becca, demanded I bring her to Stone Mountain to speak with her friend, for she feared for her safety."

My sire still does not look convinced of my innocence. Then again, my behavior in the past has been less than honorable at times. Thus he has wisely learned to be suspicious of my motivations.

"Should I have refused a direct order from a queen?" We both know there is nothing a male can do to earn the ire of other males more quickly than not following the commands of a queen. My sire has managed to drive that point home enough times that we both know refusing her was not an option.

Tucking his wings neatly behind his back, my sire straightens to his full height. "You brought her down from your keep. Care to explain why you took her to your personal space instead of our communal space where visitors are normally hosted by our clade?"

All the fight leaves my body, for we both know there is no excuse for such behavior. Turning, I leave off attempting to explain things I do not yet fully understand myself. My sire wisely leaves me to my own devices for the time being, but we both know this is not the end of this conversation. If I am certain of anything, it is my sire will eventually get the answers he seeks from me.

Instead of returning to any kind of productive work, I hover high in the trees, spying on my new queen. I know not why this particular queen holds such fascination for me. Is it like my sire said, she physically resembles the queen of my dreams? Or is it because she is fierce in protection of her friend and her voice is easy on my ears?

Get the hell outta here until you can control your mating scent, 'cause I'm not interested in smelling it. Her angrily spoken words float through my head. She did not say she didn't like my mating scent, only that she did not wish to smell it at that moment. Perhaps I am delusional, but I chose to think that means she is open to being exposed to my scent at some future point in time.

I like observing her. When she demanded that I leave my own keep earlier, I spied on her from a nearby canopy in the trees. When I saw her touching all my most prized possessions, I should have felt furious. Instead I felt a certain fondness grow in my chest for this perfect queen. With each new item she touched, she became more mine and less everyone else's.

I quickly hatch a plan to feed her from my plate and have her use my personal eating utensils. The thought of my spoon being inside her mouth makes my cock swell. Her lips sipping from my cup will make every inch of her mine. The fact that none of that makes any semblance of sense doesn't bother me in the least, for I am deep in some fantasy of my own making. This fantasy in my head is a powerfully compelling one, where this lush and headstrong queen grows to worship me and asks me to be her protector. But why stop there? In my mind, she loves my mating scent and insists upon rubbing her soft body all over me. Yes, I'm enjoying this vision in my mind so much I can't stop.

Once I put my nose between her soft thighs, my dragon will awake and then, we will mate her. I know the human queens can breed for our weaker brethren, but I do not know if those of us with older and purer bloodlines can breed them. Though the thought of her, heavy with my young, flares my lust, I will settle for breeding for her if that is what must be.

I will admit that I have thought to avoid mating, but this one is perfect, and she fell right into my lap. Surely, she must be the most desirable queen in all the land. Her hair blows freely in the wind, long and full. I like the way her soft ass moves when she walks. It's practically obscene. When she laughs, her full breasts heave and jiggle in the most alluring manner. I know very little of her disposition, but her body is something I would never tire of gazing at.

Leaning closer, I remind myself that getting lured in too quickly by a female's queenly charms is not advisable. I will keep her close and try to learn as much about her as possible. I'm confident that after touching all my prized possessions and being in my bed, enough of my scent lingers on her body to warn off other males.

There is very little doubt in my mind that if I hang onto her, she will choose me. I'm larger, stronger, and have a more valuable hoard than everyone else, so naturally she will attempt to mate with me. Since I know little of human queens, this all makes perfect sense to my mind.

My spawn-mate's new queen continues to be just as

annoying as she ever was. She's loud, squealing her delight in a pitch that hurts my ears. She brays her complaints just as loudly. Not my prospective queen. Her moments of joy are quiet and guarded. I can barely make out her words on the wind when she speaks. Where Narcis' new queen is garish and her hair bright, mine is unobtrusive, and her hair is the color of burnished metal. This queen can be fierce if need be, but she has many fine qualities. I find myself admiring her inner strength and the way she carries herself. The longer I observe her, the more I wish to make her mine.

Still, selecting a mate is not a decision to be taken lightly. I should remain aloof and hold back until I am certain she is a good match for me. Of course I won't let any other males around what might become mine. That goes without saying.

A branch near me rustles slightly as Val lands. I know it's him because of his scent. "Back from licking your wounds so soon, my spawn-mate?"

"Why are you such an unmitigated ass?"

"No idea. Did you talk to Narcis?"

"I've got nothing to say to him."

"Bet you're glad you didn't share your hoard with her now, aren't you?"

He snorts a laugh. "Yes." There's a short pause before he speaks again. "I've been thinking about sniffing around that decadent new queen you dropped off."

"What?"

"Aren't you the one who always said humans are weak and mating them would dilute our ancient bloodline?"

I never said that exactly, but he's not far off. In any event, that was before I met this Queen Becca. "Get within a hundred paces of my new queen, and I'll drop you where you stand."

He chuffs out a wheezy laugh, and I realize he only dropped by to have a little fun at my expense. His next words make me want to remove his head from his treacherous body. "Her scent calls to me, Argon." It's the traditional phrase our people use when they've scented their mate.

I growl a warning low from the back of my throat. "That makes two queens you've mistaken for your mate. Better get your ridiculous snout checked out by the healers, because something is clearly broken."

"Want to know something strange?"

"Stranger than being drawn in by another's mate? Sure, tell me stranger than that."

"They all smell delicious, except a handful. Why would some few of them be scented differently?"

"Different how?"

His nose crinkles in distaste. "Like they are made of pure evil."

Shock shoots through me, lodging in my gut. "You mean their scent is like the Draconian queens of old?"

He nods without giving me eye contact. My mind swirls with a million different worries. I refused to allow myself and my family to be subjugated by the Vithacan parasites again. Once they get a foothold on one planet, they quickly dominate every male and kill every rival queen. Our clade barely survived the rule of Draconian queens who were infected with the Vithacan parasites.

"We now know our former queens scented like their Vithacan parasites. If what you say is true, you must speak to our sire without delay. The safety of our world depends upon your telling what you know. You must make them understand the danger we're in."

His voice is heavy and tinged with sadness. "I was afraid you were going to say that."

"Until getting distracted by the fire-haired queens, your sense of smell has been sharp. If what you're saying is true, we must investigate now. A delay could risk the parasite spreading."

"I'm convinced to speak. Wish me luck as I try to explain this to our sire and the other elders."

"Force them to take this situation seriously, Val. I will watch over our queens and keep them from the others until this is sorted."

He gives me a distracted grunt before jumping down to glide to the ground. I watch him head back towards the entrance to our common space. Worry twists in my gut at the thought of this delightful human queen being infected. My wings jerk as my protective instincts rise to the fore. I'll not let anything happen to this queen. Protecting her life becomes my new imperative. It is as if Providence has brought her to me. I have never been a male to shirk my destiny.

ALL RIGHT, SOMETHING REALLY STRANGE HAPPENED while Willow and I were visiting this afternoon. There was a flurry of activity and dozens of dragon warriors stormed into the area. There was no fighting, just lots of back and forth conversation we couldn't quite make out.

Both of us were quickly whisked away and placed into seclusion. I don't know what's going on or why we can't at least wait it out together. Their behavior makes me think this world might be under some kind of threat. I remember on Earth the royal family never traveled together for fear of losing them all at once. If there is great danger, I could see the Draconians not wanting to lose two queens in one fell swoop. It's the only reason I can think of why they might insist on separating us this way.

Wringing my hands in my lap, I pray we're not under attack. When nothing happens after a couple of hours, my anxiety clicks down and I find that I'm more bored than afraid. I need to piece together what's going on, so I peer out over the ledge and monitor the situation below.

Eventually, I sit on the ledge of Argon's cave home and

swing my feet over the edge. Although we didn't introduce ourselves, I know that's his name because it's what the older man called him when he came out spouting angry threats. For some reason, he's not allowed to have a queen of his own. Maybe he's too volatile or not high enough in status. It's a real shame because he's kind of hot.

By gazing at the activity below, I can make out people walking briskly. They're talking and waving their arms around before going into the mountain. After a short while, they leave. Warriors keep landing, talking and then flying away. Every time I think things are slowing down, a bunch more land. I'd give anything to hear what they're talking about. The not knowing is killing me.

At least I got the scoop on Willow. She has a major league crush on Argon's brother and insisted upon having a look at his place. I don't think she realizes how far from the city these guys are. She dropped her com device while swinging on the vines and then got distracted by her new guy. That's why she didn't contact me.

I'm not angry she left me hanging. I know she's young, a little high strung, and a lot impulsive. She's got some amusing stories about this small group of males. She says the older man is their father and his four sons all live here. I don't know why, but she argues a lot with her guy and catches some aggravating looks from the others because of it.

The big surprise is all the arguing back he does. I've never met a Draconian male that will even disagree with a woman. The ones who live here are different to the point of being difficult at times, according to Willow. To my mind, that makes them worlds more interesting than the ones who just mindlessly agree with everything you say. Even Argon is more mouthy than any Draconian I've ever seen.

I spy more movement below. Whatever is going on is between one of Argon's brothers and the visiting warriors. All the other males in his family are perched on ledges up the side of this mountain in what I assume are protective stances. They want us up and away from the visitors. I feel a bit like a doll that's been put away for the day.

For reasons neither of us fully understand, we aren't allowed in each other's quarters as a general rule, not just because of the crisis. The males don't enter each other's spaces either. My best guess is these guys are more primitive than the ones who live in the city and therefore more territorial about their personal spaces.

Willow did say that the big cavern in the lower center of the mountain is the only communal space and they all come and go from there throughout the day, have meeting and share meals there. Naturally, we can't be there because that's where the visitors are meeting with Argon's brother, Val.

Why is everything about these men so complicated and nonsensical? Although it's kind of aggravating, in a way it's also exciting. In the city, anything goes. The men will tolerate pretty much any behavior out of a woman. I know because I've seen some stuff that set my hair on end. Let's just say some of the women are not well balanced. They're actually pretty bitchy.

I've seen at least one who seemed to be collecting males for her family group. The last time I set eyes on her, she had an entourage of at least eight men following her around. Some of them didn't look particularly happy to be there, either. Anyway, around these parts the men expect us to moderate our voices and conduct ourselves with a degree of decorum. They treat us respectfully, but I can tell it's hard for them to reel in their tempers at times. Smiling, I remember how Argon struggles to maintain an air of dignity. It clearly does not come naturally to him. They're not unbalanced enough for me to fear they'll hurt me but from the little I've seen they do have a hard time deferring to us constantly. Strangely enough, their behavior makes me feel more like a person and less like an object.

There is a sound similar to a trumpet, but I can't see where it's coming from. The men take turns leaving, and Argon shows up with a covered tray. I get up and move back towards the table we use to take our meals.

If I'm really nice, perhaps I can sweet-talk some information out of him about what's going on below. Some women might have pulled an attitude by now and demanded answers. I'm reluctant to do that, especially if there's an invasion pending, because I don't want them withdrawing their protection.

I know what it's like to fend for myself, and therefore I have a healthy respect for men who provide and protect. I know that probably makes me weak. But after all I've been through trying to scrape by on Earth, I don't care if needing them makes me seem lacking. The truth is my mind and body can't take much more end-of-the-world stress.

I watch from the sidelines as the huge, scarred warrior moves around his half-finished space. He pulls down plates and flatware and metal cups. There appears to be a silver set and a golden set. After spreading everything out on the table, he tugs a large ceramic jug down from a shelf along the top of the wall. All right, now he's really got my attention. I pad over, hoping there's something intoxicating in the jug. I've been in the city for several weeks and haven't seen anything approximating wine or liquor.

One gigantic clawed hand gestures towards a chair he's moved up to the opposite side of the table. I believe he's been living here by himself so far because he's only made provisions for one. Even the extra set of dishes he's dug up are tarnished and look like something he hasn't used in years. I almost smile at me using my powers of deduction to figure this guy out.

Since I'm starving, I take the seat he's offering, only to realize he's given me all the gold utensils and reserved the discolored silver for himself. This must be Argon's version of hospitality. He definitely didn't have to do that, but it makes me like him more. I can't help but smile at his thoughtfulness.

He loads my plate with a little of everything and drizzles something red into my cup. It smells like some kind of wine. God, I need a little something to help calm my nerves, now more than ever. The moment he moves away, I take a sip. It goes down smooth and immediately causes a warm glow in my stomach that slowly spreads throughout my body. I'm so grateful, I could cry. Instead I give a proper thanks to the man responsible for my keep.

"Thank you for the food and drink. I really appreciate the time and trouble you're taking to make sure I'm comfortable here." He sits across from me with a pleased expression. I scramble to add, "And thank you for the company as well. You've been really good to me." I don't tack *so far* onto the end of my statement because that would be rude, but I'm kind of still worried things aren't quite how they seem.

He speaks as he slices a large chunk of meat off with his claw. "Are all humans so polite? I'm not used to queens who dole out compliments." I watch him toss the piece into his mouth and chew.

Unsure what to say, I start babbling, hoping something will stick. "We're all supposed to be respectful. Your people welcomed us to your nice home world. Since we are beholden to you, being polite and courteous is the least we can do." I take a bite to show I like his food and quickly chew before speaking again. "I know that I can't leave until this crisis is over, so I'd like to offer to help out in any way I can."

When his heated gaze lands on me, I clarify my offer. "I'm not referring to sitting on your lap or anything like that, but I could help organize all your belongings or something of that nature."

His gaze turns warm and amused. "To do that you'd have touch everything I own."

"I'm sorry, come again."

Taking a long drink from his cup, he shows off the large claws wrapped around his silver cup. I watch the muscles in his neck move as he swallows. His chest is still bare even though it's getting colder outside, and his scale-covered muscles ripple. When his empty cup hits the table, he speaks. "I do not normally allow others to touch my personal possessions. However, I will make an exception for you because you will be staying in my keep."

Trying not to glance at his huge bed, I ask anxiously. "If I'm staying here, where will you stay?"

"I am sharing my space, not giving it over to you." His tone is growing disgruntled.

"I can sleep on the rug if you have an extra blanket."

"Aren't you a charming and innocent little queen?" Something changes in his expression. "I appreciate that you aren't demanding and ungrateful. Therefore, I will rest on the rug, and you may have the bed for now."

Something in my chest relaxes a little. I keep swinging back and forth between thinking he's relatively nice and second-guessing myself. I need to pick a stance and stick to it. "Thank you for your generous hospitality. I'm more grateful than you can imagine."

"I doubt that, my pretty queen. I am a creative male with a vivid imagination. I can imagine vast amounts of gratitude."

Squinting my eyes, I mumble, "Are you flirting with me? I honestly can't tell."

Pouring us both some more of his strange fruit-berry wine, he grins. "If I am not permitted to attempt to ingratiate myself to you, now is the time to speak up. Truth be told, I'm becoming quite fond of you."

I take another sip from my once-again full drink. Looking into his handsome face over my glass, I can almost imagine falling for this man. "Humans have a saying about biting the hand that feeds you. It would be impolite to make demands on the man sheltering me during a storm."

"You speak in riddles. I find that interesting."

Wrinkling my nose, I try to decide if he's serious or making fun of my simple way of speaking. He seems taken aback by my change of expression.

"Stop making adorable faces. I refuse to be swayed by a pretty face." His eyes linger a moment before dropping to my chest and he murmurs under his breath. "Or swayed by such a decadent form."

I take a bite of the food on my plate as I think over his words. He's called me lush and now decadent. That coupled with his invitation to sit on his lap and his heated gaze make me think he really does like what he sees. Since I don't want our conversation to stray into our mutual attraction, I ask about the goings-on down below.

"Am I allowed to know what the current emergency is about?"

His head snaps up so fast it makes me jump. His hands

move away from his plate and disappear below the table. My anxiety surges again when his expression goes blank. It feels like he's preparing to deliver some really bad news. Understanding the importance of the moment, I put down my flatware and wait patiently for him to speak.

"Our people are not from this sector of space. Where we come from, vicious Draconian queens rule with an iron claw. It took us thousands of years to realize they were infected with parasites that fed on the energy associated with pain and misery. We were enslaved, abused and our young were reaped if the queen determined they were imperfect."

My hand flies to my mouth to keep me for making a horrified sound. I had heard something about them abused by their former queens but nothing like this was listed in the database. I guess it's the kind of horror that isn't polite to write down for everyone to peruse at their leisure. "I'm sorry that happened to your people."

Taking another long satisfying gulp of his wine, he forces himself to continue. "Luckily, our queens cared little for those of us with ancient blood. We were seen as little more than animals by queens intent on creating young that were ever more humanoid in appearance." Setting his cup back down, he sighs. "We thought those days were long behind us. Unfortunately, my hatch mate scented the parasites on a few of your kind. The parasites will cause them to become increasingly cruel until they go insane."

Understanding hits my brain like a million bolts of lightning. "I've met some women who were really awful, only I didn't know it was because they were infected."

He stands so fast his chair nearly topples over. "You were in the company of parasitic queens?"

I nod, forcing myself to be honest even though things

could go very bad for me if they think I caught whatever the other women have. "I accidentally bumped into one on the street, and she shoved me so hard that my ass hit the ground."

"Were you injured?"

Shaking my head, I stand as well. "No. It just startled me, and I made a point of not going near her again."

His hand moves to his belt, and I worry he's going for a weapon to stun me with. He grabs his communications device and thumbs a message for a moment. I grow increasingly anxious until I begin speaking just to release some tension. "I'm sorry if I brought something contagious into your home. I would never make you sick intentionally. I hope you know I'm not like that."

His head lifts and he shoves the little device back into its housing unit on his belt. "Have no fear, Queen Becca, the parasite does not affect males. We can neither carry the parasite, nor be made ill by it. Even if you are infected, no harm will come to my clade."

"Thank goodness."

"Our primary concern is identifying those who are infected and removing the parasites before they can do permanent damage to your systems."

"I'd hate to be the carrier of some kind of plague."

"Have no fear. I will ensure your safety."

"What do you mean by ensuring my safety?"

"Sit and eat. A medical unit will come with a full scanner to see if you are infected. If so, our healers will remove the parasite. You have not been here long enough for it to have rooted in your system."

Although eating is now the last thing on my mind, I force myself to follow his directions. The whole idea of a parasite rooting in my system sounds ominous. Actually, the thought of having parasites that feed on negative energy makes my skin crawl. I hope and pray Willow and I are not infected. Worry twists in my stomach because I know Willow has a short fuse. Is it just her personality, or is she infected?

As if sensing where my thoughts have strayed, Argon says soothingly, "Eat, my lush little queen. You have my word that all will be well."

I nod and bring food to my lips. The conversation kind of dies, but I keep shoveling food into my mouth like he asked, no longer tasting it or caring what I'm eating. He fills my cup again and pulls out a small box. I only begin paying attention when he drags his massive chair over beside me and opens the box.

My nostrils flare, picking up the most delicious scent. He reaches into the box and pulls out a tiny sweet. It looks like a tiny pie in his huge hand. Rather than giving it to me, he takes a bite and then shows me what's inside. It looks like nuts and some kind of red fruit. When he brings the half-eaten treat to my lips, I look him in the eyes as I open my mouth. He's practically glowing with happiness as he slides it carefully into my mouth. It tastes as delicious as it smells.

He insists upon feeing me several pieces by hand until I literally can't hold another bite. I place my hand on his, stilling his hand when he reaches into the box for another. When he pulls his hand out, I grab one and bring it to his lips. If his pleased expression is any indication, feeding each other by hand is some high-level flirting in his culture.

A deep voice sounds from the mouth of the cave. "The healers are here, my scion. Please bring your new queen."

He stands and holds out his hand for me, not bothering to correct his father about me not being his female. I suspect that denying it in front of his father might humiliate him, so

I don't say a word either. When we get out to the ledge, I'm shocked to discover a large shuttle hovering silently in the air. When the door opens, a ramp slides out and touches down on the stone outcropping in front of us. The juxtaposition between the ultra-modern shuttle and Argon's half-carved cave home is nothing short of bizarre.

Argon pulls me to his side and through the door. At some point I realize his wing has slipped around the back of me, blocking my back from view of the other men we pass. I don't know whether he did it because he doesn't want them looking at me or to make me feel safer and more secure. Then again, it could be some kind of possessive display meant to signal that I'm his. Hell, I don't know, and I'm too worried about being infected to even care. I can't imagine how I'd be handling this if I weren't three cups of wine into the evening. A little voice in the back of my mind says I'd be losing my shit without the fortifying drink in my system. Extreme times cause people to over-rely upon crutches like alcohol. I make a mental note not to do that in the future.

ARGON

My scales are rippling into battle form and it's because my new queen might be infected. It might also be because I abhor having her walk among too many unmated males. I can't stand their eyes on what might be mine. It's all I can do not to bare my teeth at them as we pass.

Deep down in my soul, I do not believe she is infected because she's far too sweet and accommodating to be hosting a vicious Vithacan parasite. Since she did have physical contact with an infected queen, I will see her scanned just to be certain. The window of opportunity for discovering and removing a parasite is small. I will take no chances with this perfect female who did not contest my claim on her in front of my sire.

My dark heart is secretly thrilled that she reached out and placed her soft human hand in mine, uttering not a word of complaint when my sire referred to her as my queen. Though she might be holding her peace out of consideration for my feelings, it is just as likely that she wishes to spend more time with me. Perhaps she wishes to test our compatibility in other more intimate ways.

I tug her closer to my side and close my wing tighter around her back. All eyes continue to be upon us and I do not like it. My mild-mannered brethren are no doubt wondering about this fire-haired queen choosing to remain at the side of such a primitive male. They will all burn in my fires if they do not give us more space as we pass. My growl of warning is deep and ugly, causing my queen to flinch. It gets the others moving back though, and that is what I need to keep from exploding.

The moment we enter the medical suite, Queen Becca gasps. "There she is, the woman who pushed me down."

I see her lying on a healing platform with a stasis unit glowing over her clearly sedated body. Stopping dead in my tracks at the door, I ask the healer walking towards us, "Is it true that queen is infected?"

He glances over his shoulder before turning back to speak to us. "Yes. We are keeping her in stasis to slow the development of the parasite."

My voice echoes off the walls. "You intentionally brought my queen into the presence of an infected host?"

The healer flinches, and I feel Becca's blunt nails digging into my arm. I begin to draw her backwards through the door again. Several healers rush forward. An elder healer barks orders at the others to stay back before speaking to me. "Our chain of command has initiated contamination control protocols for every queen suspected of hosting a parasite. You will not be allowed to leave with your queen until she is scanned." The tone of his voice communicates that he will force the issue if I continue backing away. I hear several laser rifles power up. Before I can go for my own weapon, my queen stills my hand much as she did when I was feeding her sweets. "Let's just get me scanned and out of here as quickly as possible."

My hands closer around her and I debate my options. I don't want her anywhere near an infected host. It's true the stasis unit will keep biological pathogens nearly frozen and contained, but how can I be certain the healers used proper sanitation measures when examining the infected one?

Jerking my head in the direction of the healing station furthest away from the active stasis unit, I grudgingly capitulate. "Let me watch you decontaminate that unit, and I will allow my queen to be scanned."

Rather than provoke a full-blown conflict with me, they rush to sanitize the raised platform and scanning unit. Queen Becca clings to me, resting her head on my naked chest. If I weren't so angry, pride would surge in my heart because she draws strength from me in her time of need. I loosen my hands slightly so as not to bruise her, but she only burrows closer to me. I realize she's shaking slightly and worry that she might be cold. I do not want her using any of the covering from this medical unit, in case they are contaminated. I wrap my wings around her and she stops trembling almost immediately.

When they are finished, we move forward and I lift her up onto the unit. "Lie back, my sweet queen. The scan should not take long."

She lies back but doesn't let go of my hand. I squat down beside the unit and keep my expression blank so as not to alarm her further. The machine comes to life, whirling and beeping as it scans each system in her body one after another. The healers whisper but my keen hearing can make out what they're saying quite easily. They're relieved to find no evidence of the parasite. I relax a little as they scan deeper to verify their initial findings.

I rub her hand with my thumb, and she glances in my direction. I smile a little, and she gives me an anxious half-hearted grin in return. It's a start. We're learning to trust each other. The emotions blooming in my chest for this sweet queen surprise and shock me. I never thought to be so taken with a weak human queen. Looking into her eyes, I realize she is not weak, just very different. She has an inner strength I did not expect to find in a small human female.

When the scan is over, the elder healer begins asking my queen questions. He asks about the diseases her kin have had, if she has ever been gravely ill, and if she would like to be taken back to her quarters in the city.

I come to my feet so fast, the elder healer has to take a stumbling step back to keep me from knocking him over with my spread wings. "No one is taking my queen away," I roar without meaning to. Another laser rifle powers up. That makes five of them. The warriors are probably spread around the top of the catwalk where they can easily take me out without harming the others.

Queen Becca is off the table in the blink of an eye and throws herself at me. I catch her with one arm and flip my wing around the back of her so fast it knocks her lush body into my side. She quickly mumbles, "No, I'm fine being with Argon's clade for the moment."

I ignore the fact that these healers just tried to steal my queen away. Since my queen is not infected I ask the only question I'm truly interested in knowing. "How many of the humans still need to be scanned for the parasite?"

"Over three hundred and fifty are left to be examined at this point."

"How long will it be until it is safe for our females to visit the city?"

The elder healer scratches his chin. "We'll need to examine them all, track down the source of the contamination, ensure no trace of whatever contaminated these queens remains and then initiate a second round of scans to make certain nothing escaped our initial efforts. I'd estimate that by spring we'll issue an all-clear."

"We're leaving now. Under penalty of death, do not bring infected queens into our territory ever again."

A deep voice floats down from above. "Never think for a moment that your queens are more important than the others. All queens matter equally. We will do what we must for the common good."

Without looking up, I respond with conviction. "I have no quarrel with queens, infected or not. However, I will kill any male who brings them near our queens. Do not forget my words, Mathadar."

I know not if I strike fear in this warrior's heart with my threats, but he allows me to walk out of the medical unit with my queen protectively under my wing. It seems that when all the other warrior's eyes are upon her, she cuddles close to me but when we are alone, she wishes to be far away on the other side of the room. I must be a simple male because I do not understand queens. The moment we step off the shuttle and back into my keep, I predict she will move swiftly away.

I walk Queen Becca into my keep and sit her down in my throne. Unlike my weaker brethren, those of us who possess ancient blood have a huge stone chair, usually pulled in front of a warm fireplace. I drape my favorite fur blanket around her shoulders and retrieve the huge logs my sire left outside my door. Tossing three of them into the newly hewn fireplace, I breathe my fires onto them and watch them ignite.

When I am certain the fire is warming my queen, I retrieve her cup and pull down a bottle containing a beverage designed to induce sleep. My anxious queen needs to rest rather than worry about the situation at hand. Pressing the cup into her small hand, I tip it up to her lips with one claw. "Drink, my queen. It will help you rest."

She swallows the mouthful and scoots over to make room for me. Snorting a laugh, I pick her up, drop down in the seat and snuggle her up on my lap. For once, she does not complain or try to squirm away. We sit watching the flames dance for a long moment before she speaks. "You smell really nice."

Tucking her head under my chin, I can't help but smile. "I'm intentionally not releasing my mating scent, so that's all me."

She shakes with silent laughter, and I run the blunt end of one claw up and down her back. "Protecting you brings out all my qualities as a male. I've never felt so much at peace as I do in this moment."

Rubbing her cheek against the slowly softening scales on my chest she whispers, "Me either."

My slight human queen is growing drowsy. I wrap my fur throw around us more tightly and take a moment to just enjoy the feeling of this lush queen in my arms. Everything about being her protector calls to me as a male.

The healers think it will take until the spring to eradicate the parasite from our settlements. Clutching Becca to me, I wonder if in the long history of my people a queen has ever escaped after spending an entire winter in a dragon's keep. Surely, she must know that wintering with a dragon is a good way to end up mated to him. My dark heart thrills at that thought, for I can clearly envision this soft accommodating queen warming herself by my fires, luxuriating in my bed, and even riding my cock.

I jerk slightly as I realize my inner dragon is awake and paying close attention to my train of thought. We like the scent of this human queen very much and are very interested in the pleasure we think we can find with her.

He wants a snout full of her queenly scent from the place where it is the strongest, but I know now is not the time for such pursuits. She only allows me close because she's coming to view me as a protector rather than something she requires protection from. No, we will do nothing to alarm her opinion of us. Instead we will bide our time, slowly drawing her closer and closer until she opens herself to us like the most delectable of flowers. Then we will revel in all the scents, tastes and pleasures such a perfect female has to offer.

I find myself growing drowsy. Images flit through my mind of the dream I had in the cave. Cool gold liquid moves over my scales as if it has a mind of its own. Instead of questions about who I am, there are questions of who she is. I startle awake when I realize the liquid is moving over me to get to my new queen. Luckily, the images are nothing more than another nightmare. Unsure why I keep having this particular bad dream, I pick up my queen and put her to bed.

She looks so lovely lying against my stark white bedding. Her hair is fanned out against the things human call cushions, making me glad I indulged in purchasing this newest human fad. Fluffy squares are highly coveted by the humans. Therefore, I purchased them for my hoard. I move back and slowly draw her gown up her legs, stopping at the top of her boots. I deftly undo the laces and slide them off her legs.

Wondering if I dare remove her gown, I decide that this night I do not dare such a thing, for it will surely provoke her ire. I pull a heavy fur blanket over her body and set the invisible force field to its densest setting over the mouth of my cave home. Leaving the sleeping platform holding my queen is the most difficult decision I have made of late. Warriors do not sleep with queens uninvited. This is rule number one and violating it is punishable by death. Instead I go back, curl up in my throne and pour myself a large glass of ale. Wine is for the delight of queens and I will drink it, but ale warms my soul like no other drink. Is there anything more a dragon need than strong ale, a warm fireplace and a beautiful queen to protect? No, this is perfection.

DAYS TURN INTO WEEKS AND I SETTLE INTO A NORMAL routine. I sleep in Argon's huge bed all by myself while he sleeps curled up on a stack of furs in front of his huge fireplace. He banks down his fire at night and it keeps the large room relatively warm. Sometimes I hear him tossing and turning at night. He's clearly having a nightmare because sometimes he strikes out, mumbling something about protecting his queen from the gold. Goodness only knows what dreams his messed-up brain conjures when he sleeps. I often think of waking him, but truth be told, I'm too frightened that he'll accidentally hurt me when he's thrashing about.

Other than his bad dreams, everything else is fine. I feel much like an honored house guest he's crushing on. It's flattering, but I just can't see us fitting our lives together permanently. Then again, who knows what the future holds? The longer I stay, the more comfortable I become in his home and in his presence.

The most pleasant part is watching his keep take form. He spends hours each day carving with what appear to be primitive tools. Draconians in the city seem over-reliant on tech compared to Argon's clade. Their life is a strange juxtaposition of modern and ancient smashed up together to create a lifestyle that's both utilitarian and filled with beauty.

For example, the bathroom was completed shortly after I arrived. He used modern lasers to cut a huge soaking tub with a cascade type shower overhead. The lasers left behind a smooth marble-like finish. They've apparently dropped a well because he added metal pipes that carry hot and cold running water from the cavern below. Before the bathroom was finished, he carried me down there to use the restroom and take care of my daily hygiene.

I like having our own personal bathroom, not only because it's more private, but because it's styled after the rest of slowly emerging space. He carved a faint but intricate relief pattern on the walls with a multitude of recessed alcoves to hold towels, bathing supplies and glowing rocks. Yep, these guys use small glowing rocks about the size of my hand to light the interior space of their keep. You just clank them together and they emit a soft glow. I don't know how it works but Argon told me once that hitting them together caused a kinetic reaction which releases energy in the form of illumination. Anyway, the effect is soft romantic lighting.

I turn on the hot water again to warm my bath. I stretch my legs out and enjoy the luxury of soaking in this huge tub. I'm careful to turn off the water before I accidentally scaled myself. It's moments like this that I live for, times when I can just close my eyes and be.

I have Argon to thank for this and a dozen other small pleasures. He may be overly protective, a little handsy and quick to flirt, but he's never made me feel objectified or afraid for my safety. I bite my bottom lip as my soapy hands glide over my stomach and up to my neck.

The big dragon warrior is quick to laugh and loves teasing his brothers. His father gets exasperated with his wicked ways, but I think he's kind of neat. It feels like he's just that tiny bit evil on the inside, and it's enough to make him do really bizarre things in the interest of being shocking and a little attention seeking. I can't help the smile that curves up my lips. He's definitely not the kind of guy who melts quietly into the background. He's way more notice-able than his brothers, to me anyway.

I rinse the soap from my body and eventually force myself from the tub. Between the warm water and the kinetic energy released by the glowing rocks, the room is warm. They even have a unit built into the ceiling that releases a particle beam to clean all the surfaces at regular intervals. It means we never have to scrub a toilet or worry about germs or grime build-up in this room.

Okay, I might just be obsessed with Argon's cool bath-room. In my own defense, we didn't have anything like this back on Earth. Water was in extremely short supply and I hadn't enjoyed a real bath for years before I arrived on this planet. Anyway, I don't like to think about Earth. It's too depressing. Earth was my past. I want to embrace my future.

I wrap a towel around myself and pad my way across the room and into the adjoining chamber. This is what can only be described as a small powder room. There is a tiny vanity which was clearly designed for a human woman because it's too small for a Draconian to utilize. He keeps filling it up with perfumes, alien cosmetics, lotions and grooming utensils. Since this is probably a set up for his future mate, I try not to touch anything but the brush and a couple of hair clasps. Looking longingly at the pretty-colored powders, I think about the woman he mates gliding swaths of the finely pressed powder across her eyelids and cheeks. Some of them even sparkle with gold dust.

Needless to say, there is nothing approaching functional clothing. I've been wearing and cleaning a couple of gowns. I picked heavy ones, intent on staying warm during the winter months. I don't want whoever moves in here for real to feel like she's inheriting a bunch of used stuff. If not for that, I'd dearly love to try on every beautiful gown in the gigantic stone wardrobe.

It's strange how I used to think the women in the city were absurd to wear gowns on an alien world. Here, deep in the mountains, gowns seem perfectly suited to wear in a dragon's keep. It's in keeping with the rustic and castle-like decor. Truth be told, the thick plush velvet feels nice and warm against my skin. There is a stack of velvet form-fitting pants with no pockets. I love wearing them under my gown, light tights for some extra warmth. I also revel in the fit of my newly acquired knee-high leather boots. They have no heel, lace up the front and are buttery soft as well. All in all, these men spoil me beyond anything I could possibly deserve.

When I'm fully dressed, I reluctantly leave the peaceful solitude of this tiny space and head back out to his main room. The space with the huge fireplace serves as a great room, only the dragon warrior has his bed there as well.

Argon sits in his throne chair, only he's pulled it over to face his desk. Rolled drawings are spilling over the sides and onto the floor again. He looks up from whatever he's drawing, and his eyes light up. "You look lovely today, Queen Becca."

I roll my eyes because I know he's referring to the fact

that I'm wearing my hair down. I brushed it dry and used clips to pull the front back off my face. When I stoop down to gather up the fallen drawings, I feel his claw slipping through my long hair. I don't mind until I stand and see him bringing a lock of it to his nose. Bringing up one hand, I tug it free. His expression shifts this petulant one. My new dragon friend does not like being denied. I layer the rolled documents in a metal basket that's shaped to handle them. I'm careful to load them one at a time, so they don't get smashed.

Argon's smoky voice sounds off. "You're an industrious queen, always looking to make yourself useful."

Turning to face him now that my task is finished, I smooth my hands down the front of my gown. "Well, there isn't a lot I can do help out in an environment like this."

"Winter is not yet half over and already you grow bored with my company." His voice is peevish, but I know him well enough to realize he's faking it.

"There are worse problems to have in the 'verse than boredom, your grace."

His expression shifts to one of amusement. "You feed my ego with your honorary titles, little human. If you are not careful, I might just decide to keep you after the thaw."

I glance over my shoulder to the winter wonderland beyond our warm keep. There is a rather large box sitting near the door. My head swivels back around to look up at him. "You've already been out today?"

He nods as his eyes crawl over every square inch of my body. Food is being prepared down below today, but I went to fetch more firewood and another gift for my favorite queen."

My eyes grow wide. "You shouldn't have. You've given me too much already."

"Nonsense. You're my captive queen, therefore you will accept whatever small tokens of affection I chose to bestow upon you."

I honestly don't know how to deal with his generosity. Only a Draconian would spoil a woman rotten, knowing she's likely not staying with him. They derive such pleasure from caring for females. It's such a deeply rooted part of their personalities that it makes me wonder if it was programed into them right along with their dragon DNA. I mumble awkwardly "You're too much, but I thank you."

Coming to his feet, he gestures to the table. "Come, while we wait for breakfast to be finished, I will unload your supplies."

"I can't imagine what you think I could need that you haven't already provided."

"Since you have snubbed the majority of my gifts, I am questing to find ever-more-worthy offerings."

Shock tears through my chest at his casually spoken words. He thinks I've snubbed him but there isn't even a hint of anger in his voice, only resolve.

Feeling ten kinds of bad for not reciprocating in a way he values, I stumble for words to make my rejection less hurtful. "I apologize for not taking you up on your offer of intimacy. I guess I'm just not sure that I'm ready for that yet."

He stops midway through unloading the box onto the table and a small dark container slips from his hand. He catches it before the contents spill everywhere and sets it down.

I try not to cringe when his expression morphs into shock. He only struggles for a moment before working something out in his mind. Then a deviously evil smile creeps onto his face. "You think my body is the gift I refer to?"

Biting my bottom lip I nod, not trusting my foolish self to speak again. How do I get myself into such embarrassingly awkward situations?

He preens a bit, his gorgeous tail whipping back and forth happily. "Then you and I are in agreement. My body is a gift worthy of even the most discriminating of queens." Gesturing to the perpetual bulge in his pants, he continues, sounding more grandiose than ever. "My cock would be worshiped by queens the 'verse over if images of it were made public." When my mouth falls open in sheer astonishment, he grins roguishly. "Don't even think of objecting until you have borne witness to the mighty beast."

I press my lips together, to keep from laughing at his ridiculous antics.

He finally moves on from the subject of his dragon junk. I thank all the gods above for small favors, because if his behavior is any indication, bragging about his junk may be one his favorite pastimes. "However, the gifts to which I refer are the fine gowns, jewels and female sundries I stocked your dressing room with."

My eyes go round. "I thought those were... not for me."

He snorts, "You are the only female permitted in my keep. Of course they are for you." He goes back to unloading the box and I see a dozen or more clear cases of different colored gemstones along with thin gold and silver wire. I crane my neck, realizing he's brought me supplies to make jewelry. I vaguely remember mentioning how I used to make beaded necklaces as a teen. Argon is amazing in a lot of ways and clearly always eager to please.

"You shun most every effort I make to care for you properly. Gesturing to a hook near the door, he mumbles, "Even the winter coat I had made for you hangs there unworn. I worried you might be sensitive to scent of males on your personal effects. So I had the coat de-scented and touched it only with gloved hands. Still, you go cold rather than wear it."

My heart melts a little. That's about the most accommodating thing I've ever heard of a warrior doing. It's strange but adorably sweet. I step closer to him and reach out to touch his bare chest. It's a bold move but I'm rewarded for my daring when his eyes light up. Rubbing his skin soothingly, I try to explain in a way that's not offensive.

"I didn't understand those were for my personal use. You are far too generous. There are enough gowns and jewels to clothe an army of queens."

His claw reaches out to slide around the necklace Aldar's clan gave me. I see his lip curl back momentarily as he slices through the leather and slides it from neck. Without saying a word, he drops it into the fireplace.

I should be angry that he just destroyed one of the few pieces of personal property that I own. I look away from him, realizing how much self-control he must have exercised to leave that bit of leather around my neck although it scented of other males. I'm somehow not even surprised when his head comes down and he licks the lingering scent from my skin.

His whispered words provoke a wave of desire so strong I can barely control myself. "I did not think you liked my jewels, so I brought you supplies to make such as you desire to wear." I pull back, trying to get control of my arousal. He looks down into my eyes and asks, "What say you, my beautiful queen? Will you wear my jewels?"

I nod, cause I'm all in at this point. I'll wear his jewels, his gowns and all the pretty makeup he bought for me. I'll even drown myself in the fancy perfume, if only he'll keep looking at me like I'm the most important thing in his world.

When his arms come out around me, drawing me forward, it hits me hard and fast that these items I thought he was gathering for a potential mate are in fact courting presents. I can't tell him what I thought because then he'll understand his attempt at courting was so subtle that I didn't even recognize what he was doing. It must have been incredibly difficult for him to dial back his pushiness when he was trying to attract my interest.

His voice turns warm and sensual. "You accept my gifts then?" When I don't immediately agree, he cajoles me a bit with humor. "They were given in good faith, after all."

I finally manage to snap out of the lust-induced trance he's trapped me in. "Of course I accept your courting gifts." To do anything else in this particular situation would be insulting. Plus, I'm strongly attracted to this man, even though he's peculiar and downright weird in many ways. As if covering for my own errant thought, I add quickly, "Any woman would be proud to have you as a mate."

The brilliant smile that lights up his scared face makes him more handsome than ever before. I almost can't stop staring at him. As if he senses this is his moment, he reminds me of his best feature. "My cock really is a thing of beauty, if ever you wish to see it."

I feel it nudging at my stomach as he gazes down into my eyes. Now most women might find this romantic or even erotic, but not me. Something about the absurdity of our situation strikes me as hilarious. Rather than laughing in his face, I grin. "Perhaps tonight we can soak in your huge tub and play show and tell."

Confusion creases his brow. "You need me to explain my cock to you?"

Finally, I can't hold in the laughter anymore. I spills out and my nails dig into his skin as I hang on to keep from falling over because I'm laughing so hard.

He pats me on the back like one sometimes does a person who's choking, and the fact that he thinks I'm having some kind of impromptu physical ailment makes me laugh all the harder. When I finally get ahold of myself, I realize he's sat me down in his chair.

Gasping for air, I try to catch my breath. "I can explain."

"After laughing about my cock, you'd best be quick with an explanation that sooths my bruised ego, lest I beat you with my second most prized possession right here and now." The look on his face is one of humor mixed with confusion, so I know that wasn't intended to be a serious threat.

Taking a deep breath I calm down enough to get my words out. "When humans are small children, one of the ways they ease us into formalized schooling is by allowing us to bring interesting things from home to show our new classmates. We show the item and explain what's so great about it. That's why it is called show and tell."

Suddenly, he's all kinds of interested. He drops down to his knees in front of me with one hand on my leg. "I like this showing and telling. I will relish showing you my body and explaining all about mating a Draconian male." His eyes drop to my chest and his tongue comes out to slide along his bottom lip. "I will also pay close attention when you display your queenly treasures and explain the intricacies of your lush human form."

"What's with you always pointing out that I'm on the heavy side? You've got a dozen different ways to say it. You've called me plump, lush, hefty, fleshy, plum, luxurious..."

"Stop talking, or I will not be able to bide my time until tonight." He snaps his jaw shut as if he's misspoken.

"Just tell it to me straight how you feel about my size."

His hand grasps my leg a little tighter. "Your soft and curvy shape is beautiful. I have always admired the queens with more rounded forms, but you are more attractive than all of them by far." His hand comes up to slip through my hair. He holds it up in front of my face. "Your hair and eyes draw me in like no other queen has. Until you came into my life, I only saw beauty in the great metal spirals on the buildings in the city. Now their beauty pales by comparison to yours."

My throat almost closes up. This man likes me just the way I am. He doesn't wish I was skinnier, smarter, blond or even Draconian. It feels so nice to be accepted for me. Instead of speaking, I lean forward and place a series of kisses along his temple, down his jaw and at the corner of his mouth before pulling back.

"Your soft gentle kisses chain my heart to yours, little queen."

Cupping his face in my hands, I rub my nose gently against his. "Perhaps that was my intent."

When I draw back to look through the materials he's unloaded, his hand goes up to touch his face where my lips were. He seems a bit awestruck. It makes me think he might have never been kissed before. What could be such a small thing feels so monumental. I smile to myself that I value being together the same way.

ARGON

WHEN THE TRUMPET FOR BREAKFAST SOUNDS, MY NEW queen stops pawing through her new gemstone and goes to the rack to get her coat. I rush to her side, helping her slip it on. It's suede on the outside with a lining of the softest white fur to be had on this planet. It's full and long enough to cover her gown. When she pulls the hood up, I kneel to button the fastener at her waist. Her hands land on my horns, and her touch sends a jolt of pure lust to my cock.

Ducking out of her reach, I come to my feet. When she smiles up at me, I feel like all is right with my world. This small being has come to mean so much to me in such a short period of time. I remember the elders saying that the warriors who dislike the thought of being chained to a queen are the very ones to form quick and deep attachments to their queens. Such is obviously the case with me, for the thought of letting her go pains my very soul.

I scoop her into my arms and glide down to the main meeting hall. We are the last to arrive, but I take a moment to remove her coat before escorting her to the table. My sire is still disgruntled that I have a plump human queen, just like I stated I would, sequestered away in my hold.

I watch my queen's mouth turn down into a frown. "Willow is still not home? I thought she might come home today."

My sire steps forward. "She is still not well enough to be discharged from care. Narcis stands by her side at the regional healing center. It is fully equipped to meet her complicated medical needs."

My queen stalks past him and drops down into her seat. Her behavior may seem as though she is angry with him, but I know better. She is disappointed and worry twists in her gut over her friend's still deteriorating medical condition. I move to her side and drop down on one knee.

When she turns, I'm shocked that she flings herself into my arms. I move forward, picking her up and placing her on my lap. I do not wish my sire and spawn-mates to see her so distraught and emotional. I quietly tend to her emotional needs as best I can.

She tears up and her bottom lip trembles as she speaks. "Why did Willow have to be one of the infected? She's so young. Hasn't she been through enough?"

I tuck her head under my chin and hold her close. "The gods only know why the innocent suffer so, when only the strong can bear it. I would gladly bear the burden of this illness if it would cause the tears in your eyes go away."

Suddenly, she sits up and tries to pull herself together. Turning to face me, she wipes at the wetness on her face. "I didn't mean to imply that I wish you'd fallen ill instead of Willow. Even strong people don't deserve to suffer. I'd never wish anything bad to happen to you."

I bring my hands up to cup her face, much as she did mine earlier. Wiping away the last of her tears with the pads of my thumb, I'm careful not to scratch her with my claws. "Warriors were made strong so that we might suffer and die for our queens, if need be. It is the way of our people, my sweet Becca."

She turns her face into one of my palms and rubs her cheek against my skin. It's a sweet and loving gesture that I never expected a queen to render to one such as me. She sighs and I feel her warm breath drift across my scales. It sends a warm glow straight to my chest.

When her eyes find mine, I can see she still suffers. "Sorry, I lost it there for a minute. I was so certain she'd be recovered by now."

I take both her hands in mine and give them a gentle squeeze. If someone asked me what I was doing, I would not be able to explain. It is my inexperience with queens that has me looking around for strategies to help her feel better, when other males would rely upon their own mating instincts. "Never apologize for seeking comfort in my arms. I was made for moments such as these."

Shifting off the bulge in my pants, she smiles up at me wryly. "I can see that you are."

My delicate human queen slides off my lap and into the next chair. Though her face is no longer streaked with tears, her skin is pink. I know not if she is embarrassed by her momentary and cringeworthy display of emotion, or if it was sitting on my hard cock that has reminded her that I am all male. It makes no difference to me, for I find myself charmed by her either way.

I scoot my Becca's chair closer to mine in a possessive display that earns me a snort of amusement from my spawn-mates and a frown from my sire. Ignoring their unwelcome yet nuanced feedback, I begin filling her plate with the foods I know she likes best. The conversation swirls around us as my sire and two remaining spawn-mates take their seats and begin selecting their favorite foods. Once all our plates are full, the conversation turns to the greatest danger facing our people.

My sire does his best to reassure my Becca about her queen friend's wellbeing. "Do not worry yourself, Queen Becca. Narcis reports the parasite was successfully removed from his queen's body. The infection had not spread, but the healers discovered a secondary injury to one of her internal organs. My scion reports his queen made mention of being jostled when first arriving on board our ship and thinks the injury may have happened then."

My queen has not started eating yet. In fact, she's not taken her eyes off my sire. She seems to be remembering something from her time on the ship. "I remember that day was absolute chaos. We had to make a run for your ship's loading bay because there were demonstrators blocking our path. Once I made it past them, I was terrified when I caught sight of your vessel. I'd never dreamed a Draconian freighter could be so massive. I felt like an ant crawling up to your ship."

I say what comes to mind, so she will know I understand her plight. "I can well imagine how intimidating our vessel was, my queen. You are brave for finding the courage to come to us." I hold up a piece of cooked meat to her lips, and she allows me to feed her. Something loosens in my chest to have this open acceptance of my caretaking in front of my kin.

"Did you know I met Willow for the first time in that loading bay?"

I only smile down at her and press another bite of food to her lips. She continues her fascinating tale between bites of food. "It's true. We were among the first to arrive, and that meant we were pressed all the way to the back of the bay as it filled up with women and children. When I first saw Willow she was rubbing her side, and she said that she'd been shoved by another woman trying to get her kids on board, and fell into one of the waist-high compartments protruding from the wall."

I continue feeding her as we talk. "Those compartments house fuel rods and other vital necessities used to get our freighters up and running in the event we are under attack."

"Well, I wedged myself between one of them and the wall to keep from getting trampled. I can't believe how many of us made it off Earth that day. There are billions of women all trying to leave, and sometimes I still can't believe I made it."

"Strategically positioning yourself between the storage compartment and the wall was clever. Sometimes our queens and their little ones are in a panic by the time they get to us."

"Willow and I knew we were risking our lives by jumping on that ship." Her face turns up to look into my eyes and her next softly spoken words make my chest hurt. "It turned out to be the best decision I ever made. I went from being tired, sick, hungry and lonely on a dying world to being cared for by the most amazing male in the entire universe."

I'm too choked with emotion to speak, because her singing my praises in public is one step away from her laying claim to me. For once in my life, I understand the gravity of the moment.

Before I can formulate a proper response, my sire speaks. "Does that mean you will be staying with us after the thaw, Queen Becca?"

Without glancing at him, she looks deeply into my eyes.

What I see in her gaze warms my very soul. This beautiful queen truly wants me. I decide to answer for my lovely soon-to-be mate. "Only a foolish queen would think to winter in dragon's keep and believe for a moment he would let her go at first bloom."

Although my family makes sounds of disapproval, my queen's face lights up. She laughs at my greedy and possessive words. That is the moment I know deep down inside, this creature is the only one in the entire universe who truly understands me. She not only understands me, but she appreciates me as a male. This must be the feeling humans call love growing in my chest. It's strange, thrilling and terrifying all at the same time, but I wouldn't trade it for any other feeing I've ever heard of.

When I bend down, intent on capturing her lips for the first time, she surprises me by capturing my jaw in her palm and turning my head gently to the side. I like the way she handles my body. My Becca drops a soft kiss on my temple, my cheek, and the corner of my mouth. It's not nearly enough to slake my need, but I understand her unspoken words. Pressing mouths that should be eating together is rude, especially when others are watching. This queen will make an outstanding clan mother.

I permit her to lift a bit of food to my mouth. She allows me to curl my tail around the lower part of her leg without complaint. It makes me wonder what other small liberties I might take with her. I concentrate on eating without nipping her with my fangs, murmuring, "I daresay, you're slowly turning me into a civilized male."

My sire snorts a laugh of his own, clearly not thinking that is possible.

My queen asks, "Would it be possible to..."

"No, and do not ask again," I snap. She frowns, but I

know before she speaks the words what she wishes. She's clearly trying to manipulate me with her smiles and tenderness. It will not work, but I will enjoy her gentle ministering in the meanwhile.

I shove the rest of a chunk of meat into my mouth. Her voice turns exasperated. "You don't even know what I was going to ask."

"You wish to see your queen friend. I will not have you within striking distance of this illness that is befalling the other queens. The Vithacan parasites ravage the bodies of their hosts, and I will not risk your safety just so you can visit with Queen Willow. Your friend will return when she is well. Until then, let my company be enough for you."

My queen takes a deep breath and grabs the golden cup that once belonged to me. She sips the sweet wine before looking down into the cup. We do not normally drink wine for breakfast, so again I answer her question before she asks it. "We suspect the parasites are water-borne. Until we discover their breeding ground, fresh water will need to be purified."

Her face falls. "I bathed this morning. Did that not pose a danger?"

"That water is recirculated through a purification system and reused. Though it is not appropriate for drinking, we know it contains no parasites."

"Thank goodness. The last thing I need is to end up infected. You'd tear the healing center apart and worry the doctors to death."

I give her a feral grin, because my beautiful queen is not wrong. She brings her cup to my lips and I drink. My life is full where before it was empty. Perhaps she fulfills my craving for affection and attention, and therefore I no longer feel the need to shock and annoy my family. If so, they should thank her because now at least they can enjoy their meals in peace.

One glance at my sire finds him observing us as inconspicuously as possible. He is assessing us, trying to decide if I am worthy of the delightful queen who chooses to gift me with her smiles and soft touches. It vexes me that he still does not trust that I am behaving appropriately with my queen. Words fly out of my mouth before I can stop myself. "You stare at me as though you have never seen a freshly kissed face, my sire. In case you are wondering, this is my second face kissing of the day."

My queen presses her lips together to keep from laughing. She is the only one at our table who finds my words the least bit amusing. I am not particularly surprised by this, but I realize that I now have an ally and perhaps even a co-conspirator on my side.

My father frowns at me. It is an expression I know all too well. "Every time I begin to have hope that you have matured, you prove me wrong. Queens do not prefer that their males discuss the affections they share in front of others. How do you not know this?"

Rubbing my chin ruefully, I ponder the situation. He has spoken on this subject many times over the years. *What happens in the mating bed is not for outsiders to know. Queens prefer to share their affections with only the most trustworthy males. Seal your lips, lest you lose your queen.* His wisdom echoes through my mind and it takes almost no effort to pull up the memories. My sire has tried on many occasions to drive this point home to me, but until this moment I did not understand the importance of his words. Instead of admitting to my shortcomings, I circle back around to the conversation at hand.

"Where are our warriors in their quest to locate the source of the outbreak?"

My sire's attention flips in an instant. "We believe one of our ships was contaminated. It is the most likely explanation that fits all the pieces."

Rruk chimes in from across the table. "One has to wonder if the parasite thrives on some little-tread part of this planet. I am told the healers say this strain of parasite is different from all they have documented prior to this outbreak."

"Narcis reports the core team investigating the outbreak is in the process of mapping the steps of each infected queen. They plan to put all that information into the central database and discover if there is a nexus where all of them geographically crossed paths." My sire pauses briefly before continuing. "If there is no nexus, it will be assumed that once one was infected, they contracted the infection from each other. We have already purged the ships clean by running decontamination protocols."

"This feels like the evil of our past trailing us into the future." Val's haggard expression reminds me that he's more sensitive than the rest of us to situations where people are harmed. It makes me worry that he's not eating and sleeping properly. Then again, he's the one who discovered the parasites were among us again. Perhaps having that kind of first-hand contact with the parasites is bringing back vivid memories of our hardship under the rule of our old, infected queens. I'm glad I did not scent them myself. I don't want that memory floating around in my head for the rest of my long life.

I should have asked him to scent my queen rather than taking her to the healing center. That thought is dropped almost as soon as it enters my mind. I couldn't chance him making a mistake about something so critical to the well-being of my queen. Also, it's clear he does not need that kind of stress right now.

"As long as we keep our queens out of the city, off the ships, and away from other queens, we can rest assured of their continued health." This is something I truly believe with all my heart, so saying it out loud causes me no hardship. For once I am given respectful nods.

My father's voice speaks up again. "You did well by discovering the red gemstone. The one you gifted to Queen Willow has proven instrumental in assisting our medical team in healing her. I received a call from the high queen herself and assured Queen Cassandra that I would pass along her gratitude."

My head snaps up to assess my sire's expression. Surely, he jests, for never have I heard of gemstones being used for medicinal purposes, and the queen of our world has likely never known my name.

Catching my stunned expression, he nods as if to verify. "I promise it is true. They scanned the red stone and discovered it is composed of the petrified sap of some long-extinct species of tree. Apparently, they were a gigantic species that dropped huge amounts of sap once every solar."

Queen Becca interjects, "How exciting. We have something similar to that on Earth. It's called amber. It's a clear orange stone but it doesn't have properties that assist in healing. The drops of sap sometimes contain samples of long-extinct insects though." Glancing around at everyone, she adds sheepishly. "Humans once made jewelry from amber."

Covering her hand with my own, I murmur, "That was my intention for the red gemstone."

My father cares not that we established this bit of sameness between our cultures. He is far too pragmatic to care about such things. "If there is more to be had, the healers wish a cube of it."

I am happy to procure more of the petrified sap if it can be used to heal the sick. My sire is encouraging me to make use of this elevation in status by being cooperative with the healers. Contributing something of worth to our society distinguishes our clade, honors my sire and helps treat the sick, so it will be my pleasure to acquiesce to their requests. "Let the healers know that I will go this very day and retrieve a full cube or as close to that amount as possible. It is located in the cave I visited before Queen Willow joined our clade."

Queen Becca's face lights up. "A cave? Can I come with you? I used to love exploring caves on Earth. I even sheltered in a couple after the fall." When I take a moment to think it over, she grabs one of my hands and holds it to her chest. "You know how crazy sitting in your keep makes me. I need to get out and have a mini adventure. It'll be fun and the best part is we'll be doing something productive together."

I don't want to take her into the wilderness, although she would be safer by far than mixing with potentially infected queens in the city. Even as I struggle to justify taking her to the place I encountered the dust that made me sleep, my father provides information to assist me in making up my mind.

"Since you didn't mention encountering any dangerous animals, I believe it would be safe if you both wear deconta-mination suits with respirators."

His suggestion of decon suits is wise. However, the part about dangerous animals suggests he questions my ability to protect her from them. That rankles me. "There is no animal on this planet that could pose a danger to my queen as long as I am at her side."

Queen Becca takes that to mean I have agreed and gives a low-pitched squeal that's easy on my ears. She throws her arms around my neck and gazes up at me. "Your face needs my kisses on it."

Grinning like a mad fool, I lower myself so she can smother my face with a multitude of tiny kisses. Even Rruk laughs at her gleeful and carefree behavior.

My father's voice is heard again, a bit more sternly. "I'm glad the two of you find your spawn-mate's queen so amusing. You'll accompany your freshly kissed spawn-mate and his lovely queen to this cave system. We'll not risk our new queen in a wild and untamed environment with only one distracted male to protect her."

As he knew they would, his words infuriate me. "I am not weak or distracted when it comes to protecting my queen."

He drinks down the last of his wine before responding. "Good. Then you can protect your queen, while your spawn-mates carry load after load of the red petrified tree sap."

Catching his train of thought, I quip, "I hate to resort to treating my unmated brethren like beasts of burden, but their assistance will speed the process of gathering this much-needed resource."

Val and Rruk glare at me from the other side of the table, but I care not, for I have a lovely and dedicated queen gazing up at me and a hero's errand to complete. Perhaps they will allow me to name this new resource. If so, I will name it after my new queen, for now she fills all my thoughts.

REBECCA

I STAND STILL WHILE ARGON SEES MY ENVIRONMENTAL
suit is properly fitted. I'm wearing one that was designed for
a youth and it fits me nearly perfectly. He spends a few
minutes explaining how to raise the head shield and I can't
believe how serious my playful dragon is being today. Then
again, I'm not a bit surprised. Anything that smells like
danger has him shifting into warrior mode, meaning he's all
business.

I suppose it's because his clan only has two women, one
is gravely ill and the other is insisting upon going on a
wilderness caving adventure with him today. I cut him a
little slack in my own mind, because I know how overprotective he is by nature. When every fastener is tightened
just right and he's certain I know how to work the helmet
shield thingie, he steps back and begins working on his own
suit. God knows, I love watching him. His muscles flex as he
moves and I think he might be over-flexing because I'm
watching. I'm so head over heels for this man that I even
think that's cute.

Trying to get ahold of myself, I hold out my arms and

flex my gloved hands. This protective suit is amazing. It's black, and everything is form-fitting, right down to the gloves. I can move, run and jump in it without any problems. Argon smiles at me as I stretch, getting a feel for any limitations caused by the suit. There honestly aren't any that I can find.

His brothers have been geared up for ages, just watching him fuss over me before donning his own suit. I gotta say, compared to my guy his brothers are all kinds of quiet, polite and mild mannered. Their eyes even skitter away when I glance in their direction, like looking at me is considered impolite in some way. I'm slowly getting a handle on their ways. My growing confidence and knowing Argon always has my back is making my anxiety and self-consciousness disappear little by little as the weeks wear on. I've honestly never been so happy before in my life. It's humbling, in a way.

Instead of walking to the site, like Argon supposedly did the last time, we're riding a hover bike. His brothers have attached some kind of contraption between theirs. They have to synchronize their movements to keep from pulling it apart when they fly. I don't have to be half-smart to figure out it's the mechanism for hauling the red petrified sap back to Stone Mountain. I like that they've named their place something cool.

That mountain is beginning to feel like home, just like this guy lifting me onto his ride is beginning to feel like my mate. When he climbs on, I have to back up while he situates his wings. It's a little weird that he's using this flying motorcycle when he has wings and can fly himself. He's being polite because his lady has no wings to fly with, and maybe he likes riding it because it's fun.

I weave my arms through the lower half of his parted

wings and around his waist, and I lay my cheek against his wings. It's softer than I would have thought. For the first time, I get an up-close-and-personal view of his sensitive wing base. As I settle in, his tail snakes out to wrap securely around my waist like a safety harness. I'm starting to warm up to that tail and I'm thinking about getting up-close-and-personal with it this evening.

The moment we take off, I realize this cycle is really fast. He must have good vision, because everything we pass is a blur to my human eyes. I can make out a few trees and some huge animals, but I don't get enough of an image to make a firm imprint in my memory.

It seems like very little time has passed before he begins to slow down. When he stops, his tail releases me and he slides off the cycle in one smooth move. I look around as he lifts me off and all I see is a winter wonderland. Like on Earth, the snow is white. However, the sparse vegetation is deep colors like orange, blue and red. Birds are moving in the trees. I can't get a good look, but I've already noticed they mostly look like bats. Feathers aren't a thing here.

His brothers come rolling into the clearing and jump off their cycles. I like watching them together. The family resemblance is amazing. They're almost carbon copies of their father, but the database said that was normal because of the way they procreate. If I were to get pregnant, our child would carry both our features. I hope Willow survives and is able to work things out with Argon's youngest brother. It would be nice to live here, see her regularly, and for our kids to play together. If it's not to be, that's fine I suppose, as long as she survives.

Glancing around, I can't figure out why we stopped here. I don't see a cave anywhere. Maybe I'm just not looking hard enough.

Argon's gruff voice clears up all my questions. "From here we walk. The cave is about fifty paces over that next embankment. I will lead with Becca behind me. You two stay behind my queen in vedra formation."

I don't have any idea what vedra formation is, but I allow him to take my hand and lead me forward. His brothers fall behind us by about ten paces, each drifting to the opposite side of our path. It makes me think vedra formation is like a triangle with us at the top driving the group forward.

I give his hand a firm squeeze. "How did you find this cave anyway? It seems a little off the beaten path."

"I was hunting on foot and spied what appeared to be an opening between two huge boulders." The word he chooses for boulders is one that means two gigantic arching pieces of stone in his language. I get a mental picture from the language implant, so he doesn't have to explain it verbally.

My feet crunch in the snow, but I don't feel the cold because my boots and this suit insulate me from the cold. Argon's strong hand in mine is my anchor on this alien world. He leads us straight to the entrance.

We activate our headgear and each squeeze through in single file. One of his brothers stays behind to enlarge the cave opening with a laser tool. I don't like leaving Val out there by himself, but they're so casual about it that I feel stupid bringing it up. All my old anxieties come flooding back, and I worry about him being attacked by a wild animal or something equally disastrous.

Argon leads the way with his tail curled around my wrist. It's weird, but holding onto me gives him the calm he needs, while freeing up his hands to hold his light overhead and shining a smaller one around so we can see where we're going a little better. I don't mind. We travel along a long winding main tunnel that bottoms out with a cluster of smaller caves.

His deep voice issues a warning we don't dare ignore. "Don't enter any of the other rooms. This is the only one with the petrified sap."

We follow behind him and I see what he's talking about. There is a huge striation of the hardened red sap running through the walls. He moves to a part that's tall and nearly touches the floor. I move back slightly when they begin cutting out a huge chunk with the lasers they normally wear on their belts.

Now, a lot of women might find this little jaunt all kinds of boring. Not me, I love getting out, breathing fresh air, caving on an alien planet and watching my guy save the world. Well maybe he's not saving the world exactly, but he's sure saving lives by discovering this sap and making sure the healers get enough to heal the sick women who need it. I'm really proud of him and his family. They might joke and tease each other, but they also work really well together.

They haul out the first chunk and it's every bit as big as the lower half of my body. It takes both of them to lift it. I follow when they carry it out, kicking any small rocks or pieces of debris that might trip them up out of their path. Yep, I can be a team player. And today I'm throwing down like an action hero and enjoying every minute of it.

Val comes through as we're passing the other chambers and begins to step into the wrong one. Argon pulls him back right before he steps into some dark murky liquid. "Not that chamber. The one on the end." The thing is, at the moment when Argon pulls him back, it almost looks like the murky water is reaching out to touch Val's boot, just missing him. I shake my head because that's totally impossible, right?

When my dragon warrior begins walking again, he calls to me. Turning what I saw over in my mind, I rush to catch up. He doesn't like to have me out of his sight. Instead of getting annoyed, I think it's kind of hot. I've never had anyone in my life who cared if I was safe, so this is a new experience for me. If Willow's guy is just half as obsessed with her, she'll pull through by the strength of his will alone.

Argon and Rruk begin loading the huge piece onto the hastily constructed contraption they've rigged up between the hover cycles. He jerks his chin to his cycle and says, "There are belts in my back compartment."

Before he can ask, I turn to get them. There's only one button, so I push it. Inside are extremely thin filaments instead of belts. I grab them, and much to my amazement, he flips one until it glows, and it bulks up. It doesn't turn into what I consider a belt necessarily, but it looks like it's crawling around the stone, finding the best way to secure it all on its own.

Argon grins at my astonishment. "It's genetically engineered by our science team. We call it smart harness because it'll grasp anything."

I'm truly and continually impressed at their alien tech. Though these mountain men clearly love their rustic and rugged lifestyle, they don't shy away from modern conveniences. It feels like having the best of both worlds. Still staring at the harnesses, I murmur in wonder, "Draconians are very clever."

"Perhaps, but none are as clever as your male." When I don't correct him in front of his brother, his expression brightens. "I am much looking forward to our showing and telling game tonight, my precious queen."

I don't know why but my mouth falls open. I shouldn't be surprised that he's talking about our sexy business in front of his brothers because I know how he is. Still, his brazen words just make me like him more because he'll say what he likes, and he doesn't care what they think. There is something refreshing and liberating about the way he speaks his mind. I never have to worry about what he's feeling, cause he just say's what he's thinking.

Grinning at him, I nod. "So am I. You've got a nice wing base, and I want to learn all about it."

Rruk chokes out a laugh and Argon preens a bit. It clues me in that wing bases might be a secondary sexual characteristic of some sort. The old me would cringe, but the new me just shrugs it off.

Argon's happy voice draws my attention from the wiggling harnesses. "Come, let us finish this job so I may retire with my queen early this night." I slip my hand into his and we head back.

Those men cut and haul stone from all the way around the wall, and we discover still more behind the spaces we cut from. When his brothers carry out the last load likely to fit on their contraption, Argon cuts one final piece. Rather than cubed, it's large and about a hand span thick, reminding me of a windowpane. Tucking it under one muscular arm, he holds out the other hand for me. Some women might be put off by all the hand-holding, but I love it.

I happily slip my hand into his, and he stops just outside one of the rooms. When we stick our heads in, I'm shocked to discover the walls are covered with the same faint relief pattern he's carved into his walls. When I start to walk into the room, he tugs me back like he did Val. "Let's go. I do not wish you to be in any of the other rooms until I've scanned them for biological contaminants."

That a weird thing to say. His voice is also off, alerting me that something's bothering him. My gut tells me that now's not the time to ask a million questions, so I let him lead me back through the tunnel. When we pass the room with dark water, I see movement causing the water to ripple and one of the ripples turns into a small wave that lifts up. A cold chill runs down my spine. One word is whispered in the deepest darkest recesses of my mind. *Danger.* That's just my old anxiety coming back to haunt me. Shove it aside girl. Don't let imaginary worries spoil your happily ever after. Talking myself down from the ledge is just one of my many hidden super skills, garnered from a lifetime of stress and anxiety overload.

Captain oblivious pulls me out of the tunnel to our transport so fast I don't have time to really think about what I just saw. He straps his piece down on top of the others and we're speeding back to Stone Mountain in the blink of an eye. I release my head shield and let the wind blow my hair.

It occurs to me that rodents are drawn to damp places. The most likely explanation for what I saw was a small alien mouse or snake moving though the muck. Forcing myself to calm down and think rationally, I realize this is what it must have been. I cuddle up, resting on Argon's wings and just let him do the driving. He drives slower on the way back, and I watch the landscape drift by, catching a glimpse of birds in the trees and little creatures peering out from the frost and snow-covered foliage. It's really a delightful and calming scene.

This could be the rest of my life if I want it. It's a sobering thought because I never really felt like I fit in when I lived in the city. I like everything about being in the mountains though. Maybe this is a sign that I need to stop sitting on the fence and make a grab for the future I want. Hugging Argon tighter, I decide to do just that.

I do not know why I looked into the room with the dust spores that caused me to sleep. Perhaps it is because I am always too curious for my own good. Both Queen Becca and I were wearing our biohazard suits, so I have no fear of us being contaminated.

However, the dream I had in that space is so vivid, I keep thinking that I will look into the room and see the golden liquid and the walls lit up. Have I ever been so affected by a nightmare? I do not think I have.

Forcing the images from my mind, I think of the game I've been promised by my new queen. Even now her arms are wrapped around my waist and I can feel her soft human form pressing into my wing base. I cannot stop thinking of her game of showing and telling. Though I walk, talk and work this day, my head has been filled only with sharing this new experience with my queen.

If she has changed her mind, I will be supremely disappointed but will not push her to reconsider. I only wish to share intimacy with her if and when she truly desires me. I'm willing to wait as long as it takes to make her mine.

Snorting a laugh, I realize that I am lying to myself in a most grievous fashion. The truth is I want her naked and in my arms. I want her showing me her fair form and explaining all her secrets. I imagine sitting her upon my naked cock and watching her wiggle to take all of me.

I should not have drawn such scandalous thoughts in my own mind, because it makes my cock surge like a youngling coming into his first heat. No male enjoys nursing a hard cock when he can do nothing about it. She shifts behind me, pressing her body more firmly into my back. I almost groan at the feel of her moving against my wings. May the gods help me learn patience when I am in the moment with her, for I am aware that human queens do not appreciate being rushed into intimacy.

When we arrive at Stone Mountain the sun is already setting. I see my queen safely off our transport and then retrieve my new treasure. My spawn-mates will unload the stone and see that it gets to the healers, for I have a queen to care for this night. They shoot me sly smiles because of what my Becca said about exploring my wing base. I am pleased beyond measure at the thought of what awaits me.

When we touch down on my personal ledge, I set aside the slab of red petrified tree sap, still undecided as to how I will use it. Urging her forward, I begin preparing our space. Only, she now moves at my side clearly intent upon assisting me in seeing to our creature comforts. We are now a unit, whether she realizes it or not.

She busies herself, knocking the lighting rocks together in our many tiny alcoves and soon the room is glowing with a soft light. I like how she moves about our space, like she's accepted it as home.

When I kneel at the fireplace, she is there grasping a sucking brush and cleaning away the ash that has spilled. I reposition the three huge logs I loaded into place before we left and bend over breathing my fires onto them.

Her awestruck voice warms my ear, she is standing so close to me. "How do you do that?"

Turning my happy face to hers, I look down at the queen who has stolen my heart. "Even ones of ancient blood like myself can no longer breathe flames. Instead, our bodies produce a mix of chemicals that create a burst of heat so strong, it ignites flammable objects. Though we call this ability our fires, it is a bit of a misnomer."

"Wow, I don't feel that heat when we kiss."

Grinning, I reach out to tuck a stray piece of her beautiful copper hair out of her face. "Of course not. I would be an unworthy male indeed if I allowed my fires to scorch my delicate human queen." I cannot believe she has not read all about fires on her data pad. "Draconians like myself have glands encased in veins in the roof of our mouths that must be intentionally opened in order to release our fires. We redirect the air from our lungs through the veins and over the glands in order to stimulate production of the chemicals and release them. It is virtually impossible for us to accidentally release our fires onto our loved ones."

"I've seen curls of smoke come out of your nose before."

"It is the vapors coming off my glands. Unless I activate them by allowing air to flow across the glands it is not enough to burn."

Her hand comes out to rest against my biohazard suit. "I really love the way your fires smell. Does that make me strange?"

Pulling her closer, I can't keep the pleased expression from my face. "Of course not. My scent is made of all the things I am. That you are drawn to it, proves the gods created you specifically for me. We were meant to be."

Her face lights up with a brilliant smile. "You dragon warriors love the idea of divine Providence."

Eyeing her with warm regard, I murmur, "Yes, we do believe in Providence."

A thud sounds outside our door, and I know that it is our food. Reluctantly, I break away from my queen to retrieve it. While I am seeing to that task, she begins laying out our dining utensils. I marvel again at how we are now operating like a team in all things. The Draconian queens of old used us as slaves. It would never have occurred to them to consider joining us in a work task. This delicate queen seems to thrive on being my companion in all tasks. It is much different from the life I have known. Although she is weak and I am strong, we fit nicely together.

While we eat, excitement builds in my chest. I can tell by the blush on her cheeks, my Becca anticipates our pending intimacy as much as I do. It feels deeply satisfying to be desired by such a lovely being. She is smart, capable and always thinking ahead. Her graceful movements never fail to capture my notice. As I ponder our situation, I realize there is not one single thing I find objectionable about this sweet female.

When our meal is over, I dump all our eating utensils into the particle cleaning unit, and we head for the new luxury bath. I begin drawing a bath. Looking over my shoulder, I see her unfastening her clothing and pushing it back off her shoulders. Rather than finishing pushing it down her voluptuous hips, she turns and edges into the alcove containing the elimination unit.

I hear the most adorable trickle of water as she relieves herself and can barely contain my amusement. If this fascinating queen does not choose me, I will die of longing for her. While she attends to her needs, I strip off my clothing and step into the warm bath. I relax into the water, leaning against the back edge. This tub was carved to accommodate my large Draconian form. There is space for my wings and tail when I recline, and recline I do. The tub slowly fills as I await my queen.

She peeps around the corner in a manner that makes me suspect she has already shed her clothing. My heart pounds a double thump in my chest as she steps out. Suddenly, I'm made of eyes. If I'd thought she looked lush jiggling under her clothing, it is nothing compared to seeing her move wearing only the skin the gods have given her.

I can hardly breathe or think or speak, when she is showing all that one such as myself might wish to see. Her bountiful breasts bounce as she walks and the flesh about her hips barely moves, as if teasing my cock and daring me to look away. Truth be told, she is so beautiful that my eyes hardly know where to land. I wish to view every single bit of her all at once.

When I catch a glimpse of the slit that hides her queenly treasures, my cock becomes so stiff it hits my stomach. Fear of spewing on the ceiling before she joins me in the tub is the only thing that forces me to lift my eyes back up. When I gaze into her eyes, she freezes in place for a moment before relaxing. "You like what you see?"

I lean forward and rest my arms on the side of the tub. "Like is a weak descriptor for such a delightful form. I have no words fit to describe your beauty. That you are mine astonishes and astounds me."

Her hands move up her stomach and she clutches at her own softness along the way. I suspect either this queen enjoys touching her lovely form or she does so to please me. Truly, I am far too excited to care which it is. "I wish to put my tongue every place you touch."

Laughing she cups her bountiful breasts in each hand and lifts them slightly as if offering them to me. "Do your women have large breasts?"

Shaking my head, I watch her toying with the pink tips, making them become hard and pointy. How could the gods make one queenly form so fascinating? My mouth dries but I croak out a response to her innocent question.

"Our queens do not have such bountiful breasts. Humans have hyper mammary development because you nurse your young."

She tilts her head slightly as she continues handling her breasts. "Right, your people hatch their young so there is no nursing involved. You do realize that if I were to give birth to your child, I would likely nurse him or her at my breasts."

I nod again, totally mesmerized by watching her touch herself. This is much more erotic than I would have ever guessed. "I would very much like to see you caring for our young that way." Now I am feeling torn. Half of me still thinks that it would be erotic, but since it involves our young, thinking it makes me feel depraved, and not in the fun way I usually feel when I am being evil. Thankfully, my queen distracts me from my conflicted thoughts.

"Well, human women have very sensitive breasts, especially our nipples."

My translator supplies the information I have been missing so far during this interlude. The dusky tips are called nipples. The program supplies alternate terms for her mammary glands. Bosom. Bust. Chest. Teat. Udder. That last one is used primarily in reference to animals on her world, so I remind myself to refrain from using it to refer to her beautiful breasts.

I can't take my eyes off her moving hands. Her fingers are delicate and slim. Even her blunt and nonthreatening claws are adorable. I mumble mindlessly, "They are a secondary sexual characteristic, much like my horns and wing base."

Her sensual voice lowers, and the sound stirs my cock. "See? We're both learning new things today."

"I very much enjoy this game of showing and telling. However, I prefer learning my queen though touch. Will you not come to me?"

"Yeah, where I come from, you'd definitely be called a hands-on evil genius."

Her words make me smile. When her hands drop down and she begins moving towards me, I cannot take my eyes away. Instead, I scoot back to make room for her. Watching my naked queen coming to give herself to me is the most exciting feeling I have ever experienced. She slips her hand into mine. I help her into the tub and right into my lap. She spreads her legs and I feel her lush bottom get comfortable on my thighs. Her pretty hairless slit has disappeared under the water for now, but I will see it before the night is out, so I do not complain.

When she looks up at me through her long eyelashes, my breath catches in my throat. I dare not look down at her chest for fear of never being able to remember words. Swallowing thickly, I ask, "Shall we take turns with the showing and telling?"

She nods and relaxes a little in at my suggestion. She seems pleased that I am not waving my cock in her face or trying to grab onto her. Now that this skittish queen is on my lap such thoughts are suddenly unthinkable. My own arousal will always come second to her pleasure and her need to feel safe with me.

I hold out one arm and slap my scales. My green scales harden for a hand span in every direction. Her eyes lift from my scales to search my face. "Those of us with ancient blood, have two forms. When we are not under siege, our scales are soft and pliable. When there is danger near, our scales harden to make natural body armor."

Her hand comes up to smooth over my scales. She stops right at the edge where my hardened scales flow into softer ones. Her expression shifts from amazed to pleased. "I read about that in the data base. It's even more interesting seeing it up close."

"My body does not offend you?"

Her eyes jump up to mine again. "Of course not. I think this is a really handy defensive feature to have. You're really fortunate because it makes you more difficult to kill." A slight smile curves up her lips and she tells me something I did not know. "The number one item on my list of desirable qualities for a mate is that he's hard to kill."

"You jest with me?"

"Maybe, but I still like that quality about you. You have to admit that being difficult to kill makes you massively more valuable as a mate."

"Yes, it does." The pride in my own voice is clear, even to my own ears. "Your turn, my queen. Show me something special about you."

Her hands come up to run through her hair. "I noticed that Draconians don't have hair."

"Some do, if they were heavily bred with humanoids. None in my clade are so gifted."

"Well, red hair is relatively rare among humans. Less than two percent of our population has any shade of red, and even fewer have auburn, which is my color."

"Alburrrn." I taste the word on my tongue since there is no equivalent in our language.

"I know how much your people love redheads. I used to

get stared at all the time in the city. Willow and I joke a lot about it."

"Our elders told stories of humanoid females with long fire-colored strands growing from their heads. It is said they fought with the aliens who manipulated our bloodlines, angry with them for making us less. Once we shifted effort-lessly from humanoid to dragon form. Because of what was done to us, we no longer have that ability. Rather than locking us in a cage, our captors locked us in our humanoid form for all times. They paid for that mistake with their lives when the fire-haired queens came to our world."

"Wow. Are you saying they were human?"

"I do not know. I always imagined their hair to be more like the fine filaments that move of their own volition and bulk up when they need to secure something important... like perhaps a mate."

She grins at my fanciful description. "I'd like to see a woman like that myself. She sounds pretty awesome."

"It is said the fire-haired queens all died protecting us, but they killed our captors as well. We have a mountain on our home world where none go. It is said the ship that brought us to that planet still resides there, rusting and decomposing because it is exposed to the elements."

"Wait. What are you saying? That your ancient ances-tors were captured and brought to your original home world in Exion space?"

Nodding, I take a deep breath. "We know not from whence we came. For all we know, perhaps our captors forced a wormhole and took us there from this sector. All I know is that I am pleased to be here in the Naxis with you."

She looks pensive for a long moment before speaking again. "I don't know if it's possible, but we have legends of dragons from ancient times on Earth. They were never said to have shifted form, but they were huge fearsome beasts that roamed the skies looking for gold." My adorable female uses her hands to gesture a dragon flying through the air, as if it is a concept I am totally unfamiliar with, and it requires a demonstration. If any other female did this, I would likely be offended. However, I find I cannot find it in my heart to find fault with my sweet queen.

When she is finished with her story of dragons, castles and knights, I nod. "That sounds much like the tales of my ancient ancestors, only we could shift forms. Those of us with strong bloodlines covet gold for our hoard even to this day. Though I cannot imagine killing for it, I would harvest it myself and work it into fine ornaments and useful items for my keep."

She smiles up at me, and for a moment I even forget she is naked in my arms. "You're making a really nice home here. I like the designs you've carved into your walls and furniture."

Sliding my hand up to cup her generous ass, I tease her gently. "I cannot believe that hard stone is very comfortable for your soft form."

She laughs, falling forward until her hands are touching my chest. "I usually just sit on a cushion."

Cocks are better than cushions for queens to sit upon. Even though my dragon wishes me to tell her this, I do not. Spoiling our moment of bonding seems wrong to me, for I do not just want her body. I want her affection and admiration and respect more than I have wanted anything in my entire life. Therefore, I will do nothing to endanger our shared intimacy.

THE MORE WE TALK, THE MORE STRONGLY I COME TO believe that Argon is my one. Before, I thought of him as a hot alien that I could trust to look out for me, and someone I thought was fascinating and different. Now, he's so much more. Once he let down his guard with me, I got to see a whole new side of him. I've been looking for someone who's honest and trustworthy. Argon is both of those things and more. He genuinely likes me and isn't just out to score a mate like the others.

Sitting here naked on his lap taking about everything under the sun is the best experience I've ever had with a man. "Now that you know all about red hair, it's your turn to share."

He bends his head down slightly and shows me his horns. "Our horns were once proud and strong. Now they move slightly from front to back and are linked to our mood."

"When I touched yours, you pulled away." I remember thinking they must be sensitive, and I got the vibe that touching them was arousing for him.

"I did not wish to have a throbbing erection while in front of my sire. Males who cannot control their bodily functions are thought of as less than among our people."

I boldly wrap my hand around one of his horns and close the other hand around his throbbing cock. I stroke them both at the same time. It is a brash move and one I didn't plan. I'm rewarded with Argon turning to jelly in my hands. His hips jerk, so I let go of his horn to concentrate on his dick. It's ringed in places and has bumps that would probably feel pretty amazing if we were having full-on sex. I use some of them to grip onto as I tease out his pleasure.

His head has slipped back, and he's looking at me through slitted eyes. His top lip is pulled back and it looks almost like he's baring his fangs at me. I know it's just a sexy snarl, so I squeeze harder and move faster. Everything about his response thrills the hell out of me, right down to the claw marks he's leaving on the sides of the stone bath. He switches gears like a pro, going from polite to almost feral in the blink of an eye.

I don't know why I'm so intent on jerking him off. Maye because he's been sitting here like a good little boy, making polite conversation while sporting an erection so hard it's got to be uncomfortable for him. He's only just now begin-ning to release his mating scent, and I'm guessing it's an involuntary reaction to how I'm handling him. Then again, it could be that I just want to touch him.

I think briefly of riding him. The problem is, he's ginor-mous and although I'm pretty turned on, my body is not anywhere near ready to accommodate this man's cock. It's not a problem for long, because the moment I brush my thumb over the tip, he shoots all over my chest like a freaking geyser.

One look at his seed on my body has his face contorting

into a mask of remorse. He makes a move to get up. "I've soiled you. That is no way to worship a queen."

I throw myself at him, pushing him back into place. Cupping his face with my hands, I give him kisses on his face. "Don't worry about it. I love having your spunk dripping down my body."

He chuffs out a disbelieving laugh that almost sounds wheezy towards the end. "The gods do not like liars, my generous queen."

If there's one thing I'm good at, it's making my guy laugh. Lying in the warm bath, draped over his gorgeous body, I make myself comfortable. His hands come up to rub my back. Although I feel his still mostly hard cock trapped between our bodies, something probes at my slick folds. It takes me a second to realize it's his tail. I look up to find his mischievous expression is back with a vengeance.

I reach around and grab it with one hand. When it's firmly in my grip, I bring it around for a closer look. It's heavier than I thought it would be and more muscular. I run one hand over the green scales before flipping it over to examine the underside. When I run a finger over the soft connective tissue there, Argon makes a noise in the back of his throat and his body trembles. "How can you be sensitive here when I've watched you smack a tree with the end of your tail?"

The tail closes vertically in my hand. "I close it before bludgeoning something with my tail." When he relaxes his muscles again, it falls open in my palm once more. He's looking ten kinds of turned on again, but I'm curious about how sensitive this part of his body is and if the sensitivity is sexual in nature. Leaning over, I blow across the tender part. His cock jerks between us. "I will not come without permission again, my queen."

I can't help but smile at his softly spoken vow. My flippant and normally mouthy dragon warrior has been replaced with one so docile I hardly recognize him. "Human women don't care about having all the power in bed. I like seeing you enjoy the pleasure I give. Watching you come is going to be one of my new favorite pastimes."

Without taking my eyes from his, I bend down again. This time I run my tongue over the row after row of tender, scale-free skin along the very tip. I taste myself a bit because he poked me with his tail but mostly, I just taste delicious male. He grabs his cock and jerks it to the side. When he comes on the side of the tub, I realize that likely would have hit me in the face at this angle.

Coming didn't decrease his enthusiasm for the tail action. Now he's practically rubbing the tip across my tongue as he writhes in pleasure. I hear a groan that sounds more like a moan, and he finally snatches my new play toy away. It takes him a second to catch his breath before he speaks. "You should be ashamed of yourself for making a proud warrior moan like a female, but I somehow doubt you are."

"Oh sweetheart, I'm not only not sorry, but I plan to do that every chance I get."

His tail wraps around my waist, dragging me closer. "Time to show and tell me all about your queenly treasures, my sweet. I wish to put my mouth on you as you have me."

Oh, I like the sound of that a little too much. Even his brutal fangs don't stop me from wanting him that way. Like the eager woman I am, I quickly scoot back and lean back on my hands. I rest my legs on either side of the tub and display everything God gave me.

Argon begins at my face and slowly trails his eyes down, enjoying every bit of me until he zeros in on my sex. Something in his eyes lights up. "You are more beautiful than I ever dared to imagine in my wildest imaginings." Bringing one trembling hand up to rest on my lower stomach, he covers my clit with his thumb. "I studied the three-dimensional images of human queens. They were thin and not very arousing, but I learned about the clit and your x spot. Human queens are to be licked until they come, and then covered. Is that correct?"

I nod, way more excited by hearing about his crude training than the situation warrants. I know they sometimes refer to sex as covering but they also use the word to mean protect. He's using it to mean full-on sex. Since I don't know anything about an x spot, I assume he means a g-spot. At this point I'm willing to take a little on faith. "Yes please. I read that your people call the licking, "the Revidian." Sign me up for all that."

He smiles at my playful banter, but then something in his expression sobers. "If you select me for your mate, I will do all within my power to ensure you are safe, protected and well-loved."

A short silence spins out between us. Words pop out of my mouth that my brain didn't necessarily choose. "Consider yourself selected, then."

Yeah, I know I'm doing all kinds of seemingly impulsive things today. The thing is, I've been thinking this over the entire time I've been here. This man has snaked himself right into my heart, and I want him now and forever. At this point, he smells fantastic, and I don't want him looking at other women, thinking about other women, or putting himself out there for them to even think for a moment that he's single. I'm locking this deal up right damn now.

Sliding his hands under my ass, he licks his lips. "Remember you said that when the sun rises, my queen. For

I have no desire to be embraced in the darkness and then forsaken in the light of day."

I sit up straight as he literally lifts me up to his mouth. He whispers the word, "Revidian," reverently as he positions me in front of his face. I drop one knee on each of his shoulders and he presses my pussy to his lips. For lack of better options, I grab his horns and hold on for dear life. They're standing straight up on his head, and he groans when I grasp them.

The minute his tongue swipes over my clit, I'm lost in the pleasure he gives. His touches are not tentative or exploratory. It's like he's practiced on one of the three-dimensional models and knows exactly what he's doing. His fingers dig into my buttocks to hold me closer. His thick tongue traces along my folds zeroing in on my clit. He begins with a firm lick and then then teases with little round circles until I'm moaning his name.

At some point he stops long enough to release an ear-splitting roar. "Out." Glancing over my shoulder, I see a shadow move to the side and slip away from the mouth of the cave. I don't know who'd be quite crazy enough to interrupt a primitive dragon warrior when he's mating, but it doesn't matter because now they're gone.

I stroke his horns, murmuring soothingly. "It's just us, baby. Come on, your queen needs you."

His head tilts up so his eyes can catch mine. I see his anger ebb away as he searches my face. I press my hips forward and I swear his body twitches with need as his tongue hungrily snakes out to taste me again. Within seconds, he's back in the zone, and I've never been more grateful for an enthusiastic partner in my life.

Since shoving a claw-tipped finger inside me wouldn't be pleasurable, the tip of his closed tail spears me. He sucks on my clit and twirls his tail until he hits my g-spot. I throw my head back and come so hard, I think my eyes are going to roll back in my head permanently.

Before I can catch my breath, we're out of the tub and he's pressing my back into the bed. Something about his huge muscular form looming over me with his wings flared out and the silhouette of his horns flips all the right switches for me. I wrap my legs around his waist, fully intent on letting my dark dragon take all the pleasure he wants from me.

Just when I'm at my most needy, he freezes. His expression is intense, and his thick cock is lying heavy on my stomach. He's perfection, right down to his pointed ears. I want him so much it hurts but he's not moving.

"What's wrong, handsome?"

"Breeding is a sacred act. I will not breach a queen without her leave."

His turn of a phrase is odd. It takes me a minute to figure out what he's trying to say. Then it hits me that he wants to verify we're on the same page about going all the way. "Breed with me, Argon. I want you." Using his word for sex makes his face light up with primitive lust.

His nostrils flair slightly as he gazes down at me. There is such raw need reflected back at me that I want to do any and everything to appease his lust. I lower my voice and try to be reassuring. "I want it all with you. Give me a proper breeding. Just start slow and allow me time to adjust to your size."

One word escapes his lips on a whisper. "Breeding."

He moves back so fast, all I see is a blur. His expression is nothing short of thrilled. I know I shouldn't be, but I'm surprised when he grabs my ankles and pulls me to the end of the bed. Staring down at me, he says. "Prepare to be properly bred by your dragon warrior."

I sit up and reach for him. When he holds out his hand, I slip my hand into his and allow him to pull me to my feet. This man absolutely loves it when I do his bidding. Something about putting my hand in his and allowing him to lead does it for him every single time. It's like it means something to him that I can't quite comprehend. Since I'd do almost anything to please him at this point, I don't hesitate or think twice about it.

When I'm on my feet, he scoops me up in his arms and strolls across the room. Reaching up to a stake that he's pounded into the wall, he lifts off a handful of the thin gripping filaments and my mouth falls open. This man is not going to tie me up like cargo, is he?

He unwinds it, flinging the two ends and dangles them right above my wrists. I'm shocked when they begin to reach for my warm skin and twine themselves around my wrists. They're binding me, but that's not enough for him, they're also snaking down my arms and crisscrossing my torso under my breasts, pumping them up.

He lifts me to drape my wrists over the metal stake. I grab it between my hands and hold on for dear life.

Meanwhile he's caught in some kind of trance. He's smiling and his eyes are watching the filaments continue down, twining around my rear and down my thighs to my knees. The filaments are so soft, and they've bulked up to cushion my body. I stretch out, testing his weird alien version of shibari. It's really comfortable, and I'm supported all the way down my body.

I gasp when he nudges my legs apart and the filaments tighten as if they know what he wants. When he's standing between my legs with one meaty hand wrapped around the restraints on each hip, I know that I am about to receive the proper fuck I asked him for nicely.

There is no way my feet would touch the ground if he dropped me, but I trust Argon, so I don't squirm or complain. His hands caress my waist gently with the underside of his hands. I'm totally at his mercy, and never felt freer a day in my life.

I would not have expected this to be comfortable, but it is, and it's different. And I do so love interesting new experiences. I don't know how I feel about being stretched out like a virgin sacrifice, but I can see in his face how this is turning him on. Since I want him to be scorching hot for me, I relax into his hold. This feels like some kind of important mating ritual for his kind, so I want to be respectful. Instead of being turned off, I'm growing more excited by the minute. He's looking and knows that I'm dripping wet, and I'm ready for whatever he wants to do.

Letting go of the ropes, he slides an arm under each leg, grabs my buttocks and splays me open even wider. With a shift of his hips his cock slides effortlessly through my folds, colliding with my overly sensitive clit. Just remembering how his tongue wrapped around it doubles my need. I whisper his name and his eyes jump to mine. We realize how on the same page we are about this.

"Tell me again what you wish of me, my queen." I can tell by the husky tone of his voice that he likes hearing me ask for his cock. Wanting this to be as good for him as it is for me, I reply breathlessly. "I want your cock. It's all I've ever wanted."

His hips buck against me again and full-length slicks across my clit. "Please baby, don't make me beg."

His top lip peels back like it did when I was stroking

him off. He growls, "You wish for my cock? Then you shall have it."

He releases his mating scent and the full force of it is overwhelming. A stab of want twists in my gut and I gasp. But Argon sees my need; no he's counting on it. The tip of his cock notches in place and he rocks forward, lifting me slightly to get the proper angle. When he begins to press forward, his expression seems surprised.

"You are not of my size."

I arch my back to push against his cock. "I am. I promise. Don't stop. Just go slowly."

He sucks in a shaky breath and swallows thickly before moving against me again. I force my entire body to relax except my hands. He rocks until he's in, and then his tail comes up to smooth down my cheek. That's the last thing I expect. I'm starting to have questions about the mobility and reach of this particular appendage. It seems to show up everywhere when I least expect it.

"Are you well, my beautiful queen?"

I nod and he shifts my body downward, bringing his wings up to cradle my body. The force of gravity drags me down and my body accepts the rest of his cock. We seem to slide into place with a wet squelch. His tail slides down and between my legs to stoke my clit. I'm starting to think of it as his best feature.

His hand strokes down my body as his wings lift me slightly. I give him a quick smile and a nod, and he begins to move. His hips pull back and surge forward with the sensual grace of a dancer. Truth be told, I love his dark erotic dance. I breathe deeply of his mating scent and watch his face get lost in the pleasure flowing back and forth between us.

I can feel every inch of him, like I'm stuffed with his

cock. Each slide lights up my pleasure receptors, making me moan. He quickly learns what turns me on most, and then goes totally overboard doing it. He doesn't let up until I'm screaming his name for the third or fourth time. When he comes, I feel it, hot, wet, and wonderful.

Instead of taking me down and putting me to bed, he pulls me down and walks me over to the ledge. He sits with me on his lap and wraps a fur around us. His legs swing over the cliff and I turn slightly to look out over the breathtaking white winter landscape. The snow is falling softly to the ground and the planet's two moons are shining brightly in the sky.

I wiggle to get comfortable on his cock that is still buried deeply in my core. His eyes find mine and he gives me a sexy smirk. "I wouldn't have taken you for a queen with quite so much stamina. Are you ready for more so soon?"

I try not to laugh. "Not a chance. I'm just getting comfortable on my new perch."

He snorts what might be a laugh and pulls me closer to his chest. "I am both proud and pleased to be chosen by a queen such as you." His jaw snaps shut so forcefully I hear it click. Something's eating at him and I want to know what.

I use some levity to lighten the mood. "What's got you worried? Speak now or forever hold your peace."

"I wish to know how many males you plan to collect for our family unit, and if you plan to breed them all."

I sigh because we've danced around this question before, and I've made it pretty clear I'm not interested in a bunch of men. Knowing Argon the way I do, he'd probably rip apart any man he found in his space or touching his mate. "There will just be us until we have young. Then it'll be you, me and our little ones."

Pulling me back he looks down into my eyes. "Human

queens prefer to breed one-to-one, but some take more than one male. I didn't know if you were serious about having only one, or if you just said that to lure me in."

I cup the bottom of his jaw with both hands to keep from letting the warm blanket slip away. "I want you to know something really important now that we're mated. Honesty is of critical importance to me. I would never intentionally lie to you about anything, and I expect the same respect in return."

"What are your other rules for me? I wish to know your expectation so I will not transgress."

Tracing his bottom lip with one thumb, I notice some pink marks around my wrists from the straps he used to restrain me. My head snaps around to the stake in the wall, and for the first time I realize the restraints just kind of slithered away without me noticing. They're lying there in floor all tiny and blameless again. I rub my wrist with one hand. Rather than upset, I'm kind of proud of what we did. It was really erotic, and I never thought I'd like anything that wild. I'm fully aware that makes me kind of kinky, but I don't care at the moment.

"You are angry about the breeding I chose?"

"Heck no, I loved it." I shake my head trying to get back to the conversation at hand, but my brain is fuzzy from all the intense orgasms. "Look, the sex is great, and we've been getting along really good. You're nice, respectful, and take really good care of me. I like that you've been letting me help out more. Outside of being honest with each other, I can't think of anything else I need from you."

His expression is deadly serious. "You will not add additional males to our family unit, force me to stand guard along the wall while you sleep at night, or exile me far away, keeping my hoard for your own?"

I shake my head. "I'd never be that disrespectful to you. I'm loving on you pretty hard. That means I honestly want to see you happy."

He releases a shaky breath. "You will not reap our young?" After watching my reaction, he jerks forward with me in his arms. "I did not mean to insinuate you would do such a thing. I just wish to hear you say in your own words that our young will always be safe.

My heart aches for this man and for all that he's suffered. "I don't know what kinds of queens you had before, but you better believe that I'd never do anything to harm our young. If anyone else did, I'd . . . Argon, I think I'd kill them."

He relaxes back against the stone edging the mouth of our cave. "I apologize for allowing my past wounds to distract from our first bonding."

"I know that after everything you've been through, trust doesn't come easy for you, but please trust me to always do right by you. You and our young will always come first with me."

He looks out over the wintry landscape and after a brief pause, he speaks. "You are the chance at happiness I never knew existed. If I did, I would have come to you right away upon your arrival."

"Aww, you say the sweetest things. You probably wouldn't have liked me when I first arrived. I was a hot mess."

"You needed a warrior to understand and give you time to adjust. I wish that I had been there for you. It pains me to think of you suffering alone."

"I have a question for you that I almost forgot to ask."

"Ask anything you wish of me, my queen."

"Humans wear matching rings to signify they are

mated. What do your people use to indicate that they're no longer available for mating?"

He grins at me. "All my kin and any Draconian males in this vicinity already know you are my queen. I released my mating scent and you will remain covered in my scent for the remainder of your days. Trust me, no male who values his life will approach you for mating."

"I think you smell fantastic. The scenting is all well and good for warning off other males. However, human women don't pick up scents very well. How will they know you're no longer available?"

"You do not wish them to approach me for mating."

"Hell no, I do not."

He dips his head in a show of respect before answering. "The Draconian queens of old would brand their males. My sire still carries my dame's brand. She was very particular about such things. She branded her entire crew as well as her own young." His hand moves up to touch a crude mark on his neck.

"I noticed you and your brothers all have the same mark, but I thought it was a clan marking, maybe indicating you were all from your father's clan."

He's not looking at me and his tone has become tense again. "I will submit to being marked by you if you wish it."

"You don't sound very enthusiastic about it."

"I will submit." His voice is hollow and wooden sounding. Whatever magic we just shared is slipping away, and I can't let that happen.

I cup his face and again make him look me in the eyes. "Make me understand. I don't know your ways."

The hurt in his eyes is unmistakable. "Animals are branded in such ways, not people."

"Your queens branded you to mark you as hers but also to humiliate and degrade you. Am I correct?"

He's too choked up to speak, so he just nods. I can't stand seeing him like this.

I try to turn this awful experience into something loving and respectful for him. "On Earth, we enjoy marking our skin with different colored ink in intricate designs. It's more like art. I once saw a male with images of trees and vines growing up one arm."

His expression turns interested. "I would like to see these markings. My people wear their battle scars with pride. Some few decorate their scars by carving away the surrounding flesh and letting it heal over."

"It's called body scarification where I come from. Humans do that as well."

"I do not wish your skin carved. It is too delicate and beautiful. I also do not wish you to feel pain."

I give him a quick kiss. "Maybe you could design something fancy with our names or our likeness in it. We could get matching marks so everyone who sees them knows we're mated. We won't have to worry about losing rings or relying upon people's sense of smell that way."

"You would get my name inked onto your body?"

"Of course. I'd be proud to wear proof of being mated to you."

"We would share the same design?"

I nod enthusiastically.

"I like the thought of my name being on your body for all to see. Let me think on this for a while and I will come to you with drawings."

"You don't mind?"

"No. This is not you branding me. This is us doing it

together." He smiles shyly. "You will inspire me to create a work of art equal to your beauty."

"Where did my smart-mouthed, preening friend go?"

Coming to his feet with me still in his arms, his cock finally tugs free with a pop. "He was replaced by a fawning fool hoping to be chosen from among all the more suitable males on this planet by a charming queen with a kind heart and flame-colored hair."

I have to laugh at the longest run on sentence ever constructed. "Hey, I think I've met her before. She's really smart. I feel certain she snapped him right up before anyone else got a chance to meet him."

He laughs as he carries me to bed. We're both spent but happy. For the first time, I feel like we're on the right track. As long as we stick together, there's no problem we can't solve and no battle we can't win.

I WAKE UP THE NEXT MORNING, STILL EXHAUSTED BUT happy. Argon has let me sleep in and for that I will be eternally grateful. The sun is midway in the sky, meaning its approaching noon. I stretch, luxuriating in the feel of his bed. The room smells like sex and my new alien husband's mating scent.

Images of last night dance through my mind. Chewing my bottom lip, I roll over and look at the stake sticking out of the stone wall. Now that I'm paying proper attention, I see that it's fancier than I thought. It's got swirls and alien words stamped into the metal. The thin filaments are all wound up into a neat bundle and hanging on the stake. If someone walked in right now, they'd never know what we did there last night. The thing is, I know. And I want to do it again sometime soon.

I hold up my wrists and there's barely a pink mark to be seen. The sexy bastard definitely knows how to handle my body. It may take a few days for my normally sex-starved body to process the glut of sex we had last night but I'll be asking again in no time. I have every reason to suspect Argon will accommodate my every request.

If my belly weren't growling, I'd probably just stay where I am and read on my data pad. Then again, lying around in bed is not a good precedent to start. I need to establish a routine and I need to carve out a real life for myself here.

Instead I grab a quick shower, get dressed and pick through the food he's left for me. I find a tightly sealed carafe and unseal the top, hoping for something other than wine. The scent of pure sweet coffee wafts to my nose. I can't remember being this excited about a drink before. My shaking hand brings it to my lips and sure enough it tastes like strong black coffee. Oh my God, it's a tiny taste of heaven in the wilds of space.

Sitting in Argon's throne, enjoying such a rare treat wearing this nice gown he bought for me makes me feel like an honest-to-goodness queen.

I almost laugh at the absurdity of my situation in spite of myself. We heard that one of the warships was making a run to Earth and coming back with supplies, but I never dreamed they'd bring back coffee. I can't imagine how Argon managed to get it this far out in the wilderness. If I had to guess, I'd say it's a gift from his father.

Before I can finish my drink, Val calls me from the mouth of the cave. "Queen Becca, please. You must come right away."

Fear floods my system because his tone is panicked. "Has Willow taken a turn for the worse?" We'd heard she was getting better. I pray she hasn't taken stopped responding to the treatments.

His expression is nothing short of totally freaked out.

"No. Argon is... he needs his queen. Please come right away, I beg of you."

I run straight for the doorway and jump into his arms. He wastes no time getting me to the bottom of the mountain. In a matter of seconds, my feet are on solid ground. I see a group of males, including everyone from our clan standing with them, except Narcis and Willow.

I don't walk with dignity like I should. I run at full speed, coming to a staggering stop about ten feet away. Staring up and down the one I've never met before, I don't care for what I'm seeing. "Who the hell are you?"

Val grabs me by the arm and pulls me closer to this thing. Now I'm freaking out, too. I don't want to come closer to whoever this is. Whatever it is, it scares me. When it reaches for me, I step back barely dodging its filthy grasp. I shake my head, momentarily at a loss for words. Its dead eyes stare back at me, and something dark twists in my gut. Danger and disease is rolling off this thing in waves, but I can't be worried about that right now. Wait, if this thing is here, where is my new mate?

Searching the faces of the men standing around, I ask frantically. "Where is Argon? I want to see him right now." My chest hurts, and I'm beginning to feel a full-blown panic rising in my chest.

His father's expression becomes cautious. "Do you not recognize your own mate?"

My head jerks from the stranger to his father and then to his brothers. Valixon and Rruk appear to be about as shocked as I am. "This is not Argon. How can you even say that?"

Holding up a medical scanner, he responds earnestly. "I'm sorry to say but it is, Queen Becca. The healers performed a DNA scan. It came back a perfect match. I verified it myself."

That doesn't make any sense. These are supposed to be smart people. "Look, I don't know what's going on here, but that's definitely not Argon."

One of the healers speaks up. "We spotted him eating raw meat straight from a fresh kill. He does not speak or respond to our questions, but this is Argon."

"It's not," I say, jerking my head to the side for no good reason but to seal my lips.

The healer continues. "We think he may have sustained a head injury or ingested something that affected his brain. Our scans are coming back clean, but something is clearly wrong. There has even been talk that he was exposed to some kind of spatial anomaly that modified him on a molecular level."

"This is some of the stupidest shit I've ever heard." I stop talking when I realize that I'm all alone on this planet with a bunch of men who aren't listening. I have to dial back on the emotions and use logic. It's the only way to get through to them. "I'm telling you, it's not him."

"The scans..." His father persists in believing what the healers are telling him.

"I don't care what the damn scans say. Use your eyes, Kryos. Does this man look like your son?" We both spare a glance, and whoever this is now has a trickle of drool oozing out of the corner of his mouth.

The older man's voice sounds defeated. "He's just sick, that's all. We need to figure out what happened to him before it is too late." The older man is looking at the scanner more than his supposed son.

Refusing to look at this abomination anymore, I start pointing out what I clued me in that it isn't Argon. "His scars aren't real. Argon's scars are raised. His marks look more like skin discolorations."

Kryos steps closer and runs a finger over one of the marks. I watch his expression turn confused. The creature places his hand on Kryos, and when the hand slides away, there is dark sludge left behind. It reminds me of the sludge on the floor of the cave in the room Argon forbid us from entering. My nose wrinkles at the smell. It even smells like the damp musty cave. Something is tugging at the back of my mind, but in my addled state, it just won't pop into place.

I move on to my next point. "He doesn't smell like Argon. Your son released his mating scent just last night. How is it that I smell more like Argon after a shower than he does?"

Val speaks for the first time since he dropped me off. "He's not wearing real clothing."

I nod, grateful that at least someone else is willing to speak up. I throw in my two cents worth about the rags he's wearing. "They're more like a crude representation of clothing." Their eyes drop to the bloody animal skins he's wearing wrapped around his hips, crotch and legs. "It's a gross approximation of the finely tanned animal skin pants Argon normally wears. It feels like some alien who really doesn't understand our ways looked at Argon and tried to copy him."

A round of gasps, noises of disbelief and whispers flutters through the crowd. I just keep piling it on, hoping his family will snap out of it. "His eyes are vacant, like a newborn clone or something. I don't know who or what he is, but he's definitely not the man I love." Glancing at Kryos, I add, "And he's not your son."

Kryos accepts a rag from one of the healers and begins wiping away the smudge the brainless creature left on him."

I dig in my heels big time. "We need to find Argon and try to figure out what's going on. When did you last see him?"

As if snapping out of it somewhat, Kryos steps closer to me. "He went to the cave to source more of the red sap. That was over five hours ago. The healers found this person on the other side of the mountain range. It would have been difficult but not impossible for him to cover that kind of distance on foot, even running at maximum speed."

I point out the obvious. "Your son would not have run. He would have flown."

One of the healers grasps one of the creature's wings and gently spreads it out. The fake Argon doesn't seem to notice. "Though this looks much like Argon's wing, it is not functional."

"Are you certain?"

Bending down to observe more fully, he gasps. "The lower antoic ridge is not broken."

Kryos explains quickly and efficiently. "The antoic ridge is a small piece of cartilage that must break when the wings are stressed by lift off the first time. We encourage our young to fly at a very early age because breaking it once it's fully developed can be extremely painful. If his is not broken, it means he's never flown before."

That does it for me. "We need to find the real Argon. I'm going to put on a biohazard suit, and then I want Val or Rruk to take me there."

"They'll both go with you. In the meanwhile, we're going to continue attempting to communicate with this individual. If this is my son, we'll figure out what happened to him."

Turing my back on the confused man, I murmur softly. "Sure, you do that Kryos." Until he gets ahold of answers, the old man is not going to let go of the person some small part of him still thinks might be his son.

I can totally understand where the old man's mind is. I just don't think the guy's playing with a full deck, so I don't know how helpful he can be. Since the real Argon is missing in action, I'm not willing to waste a bunch of time on a long-shot that can't talk or fly and eats raw meat straight from a dead animal carcass.

WITHIN THE HOUR VAL, RRUK AND I ARE STANDING outside the cave. It was only yesterday that we were all here to collect the red gemstone, though it feels like ages ago. Here we are again, only without Argon. And that pisses me off. I speak for the first time since leaving Stone Mountain. "They only allowed us to come because they think this is a fool's errand."

Rruk responds bitterly, "I am not entirely certain I disagree." He snaps his mouth shut, and it feels like he's already grieving Argon. Oh ye of little faith, I think to myself.

Val shakes his head. "I think something very strange is going on, and this cave holds the answers."

He ain't wrong. The fact is, if we don't find any clues here, we're going to start a grid search moving out from this location. I'll make them call out however many warriors it takes to find him. I don't care how much they squawk and complain. I'm not that weak little worrier I used to be, and I want my man back right damn now.

"Let's do this." I hesitate for a moment. "Remember not

to go near the room with black sludge on the floor. Argon was really specific about staying away from that stuff, and I thought I saw it moving the last time we were here. It could be infested with rodents or snakes."

Val quips, "I've never been happier to follow a queen's order in my entire life." I'm honestly starting to like this particular brother.

This time, we go in armed. I pull out a laser pistol, and we activate our headgear to protect us from unhealthy particulate matter.

Rruk takes the lead. The minute we enter the main cavern we know we're on the right track. Someone has moved Argon's hover cycle inside. I'm guessing so it wouldn't be within view of anyone who stumbled upon this location. We go straight for the room with the red petrified tree sap. The room does not look disturbed. There are no cutting tools lying out or extra slabs missing. There is a thin layer of dust that does not even look disturbed.

Val whispers, "This room is exactly like we left it."

I make for the door and stand in front of the one that had the black sludge. There's no trace of it anywhere. The floor is just dusty like all the others. I squat down and give the room a once-over visually. It's got the same shallow indentations in the walls; only three of the four walls are cracked. No, all four walls are cracked but a creeping fungus has grown to fill in the large crack splitting one wall. I stand up, thinking that I'm about done piecing together clues that don't make a damn bit of sense. Nothing we've seen puts us any closer to locating Argon.

Rruk moves to stand beside me. As always, he's as silent as death. The man doesn't even make a sound when he moves.

I mutter, "It's all gone."

He shakes his head and rubs his jaw with one hand. "It might have dried up."

"Maybe. Let's look in the other rooms." I'm getting more frustrated and angry by the moment. I head directly for the one Argon stuck his head in but wouldn't let me enter. It's dark and shadowy but I spy a tub of some sort towards the back.

I stalk into the room and head for the tub. It reminds me of the one Argon has at home, only maybe more primitive. I gaze down into the huge tub and my heart stops. Tossing my laser pistol. aside, I run my hand over Argon's warm scales. Though he's not conscious, he feels alive and healthy. I turn over my shoulder and shout, "I found him! Come and help me."

Both brothers run to the tub and help me lift him out. My anxiety kicks up when he doesn't rouse. He's wearing his own clothing but has a headpiece of gold and thick bands of gold encircling each bicep. His fist is locked around a golden spear. Nothing about that makes any sense. "Call for transport to pick us up. We can't transport an unconscious person safely on a hover cycle."

We lift his limp body out, and Rruk carries him outside while Val calls for help.

"Do think this is him? It's got to be, right?" Rruk is now questioning his own eyes, as am I. I realize at some point that Rruk is muttering a prayer under his breath for his brother to wake up. He sounds almost desperate.

I run my hands up his arm and cup his face. I recognize his potent scent. He smells like leftover sex and his mating scent. Every detail is just as I remember. "Calm down, Rruk. It's him, I promise you that it is."

"If this is him, where did he get the gold clothing and weapons?" This brother is just intent on creating problems today. I don't know, but it seems like he's not running on all cylinders. It reminds me of how some people were after the fall, they just couldn't get their heads together to survive.

"Hell if I know where the gold came from. He told me once that he was really drawn to gold and liked using it to create useful things. Maybe he's been working his own find here for a while."

My mind is really working hard to explain the irregularities in this situation. Last night I felt so safe and happy. Now, without Argon alert and at my side, I'm beginning to panic again. I need him awake, safe and sound in my arms. Staring down at his familiar face, I sense the same kind of goodness I do in my husband. That means this has to be him, right? Of course it's him. Rruk and this fucked-up situation has me doubting my own senses.

I lean over and gently kiss his lips. "Wake up for me, handsome. Your queen needs you to open those dark eyes."

Rruk reaches out and slaps him across the face. My anger ignites hard and fast. Before I even think about it, I've punched him so hard in the face that his head snaps back. That's a neat trick, considering that I'm so much smaller than he is. My hand goes to my hip and if my laser gun had been there, I don't know for sure what I would have done.

Val's stern voice sounds off behind us. "Rruk move away from Queen Becca."

The shocked man scrambles back, but I'm still so angry I shout at him. "Don't you ever hurt him when he's down again. I swear..."

Val's hand lands on my shoulder. "My foolish spawn-mate was trying to force him to wake up."

My anger clicks down a notch. "When Argon's down, protecting him falls to me. Don't either of you ever touch him without asking first." I lock my jaw, knowing I'd never have approved knocking the hell out of him as a recovery technique.

Argon's drowsy voice pulls me from my dark thoughts. "We are well, my queen."

My eyes jump to his. He's staring at me as he rubs the side of his face. Since he doesn't look upset, I feel foolish for still carrying on about it. I throw my arms around him and his wings come up around me. While we just take a minute to embrace, his words float through my mind and I realize he's not making any sense. *We're fine.* He said we. I draw back and look down at him.

"Can you stand yet?"

He comes gracefully to his feet. Besides the gold embellishments he looks the same as he ever did. He's not letting go of that spear for love or money though. I realize he didn't wear his decontamination suit. He's bare chested and was vulnerable to whatever pathogens were in the cave. His leather pants and boots are his only covering. It strikes me as odd, since full winter has settled over this area.

He looks around suspiciously before taking a deep breath. "We must get back to Stone Mountain right away. There could be danger."

"What's going on?"

"There's no time to explain. We need to go immediately." He looks strange wearing the gold, but I can't think about that right now.

The urgency in his voice gets us moving toward the hover cycles. The cycles will get us there faster than the guys flying. It's pretty much a straight shot and the cycle's maximum speed is ten times faster than they can fly.

When I'm seated behind him with my arms around his waist, I allow myself to relax. My mind goes back over what I know so far. Maybe I'm just not smart enough to put the pieces together because none of this makes any semblance of sense. I stare at the strange headdress Argon is wearing from behind. I know it's gold, but it looks burnished and hand wrought rather than smooth and shiny like I imagine gold to be. He's shoved the spear into a side pocket, and he's wrapped one arm around the shaft to keep it from falling out, like he does this just all the time.

WHEN WE GET TO STONE MOUNTAIN, I'M TERRIFIED. There are dead bodies strewn all about. I want to scream but my mouth won't open. I've never seen carnage like this. The warriors are off the cycles and running towards the mountain. I'm sure they're looking for their father. I see something hovering out over the water and suddenly I find my voice. "Argon, the lake. He's on the lake."

I run for the shore and my hands fly to my mouth when I get there. Kryos is tied to a tree sticking up in the lake. His wings are damaged and he's bleeding. He can't be dead. My knees become unhinged as I watch his sons fly out and cut him down.

Argon carries him to the shore, and I scramble forward to meet them when they lower him to the ground. Val flies away to get help as Argon examines his wounds. His father is the only one who runs around fully dressed, so he has to rip his shirt to see his chest wounds.

The old man's hand comes up so quickly my eyes almost miss the motion, and he grabs Argon's throat. Then he struggles to focus for a moment before letting his hand drop away again.

I can't believe Argon trusted him to figure out he wasn't the creature in his damaged state. Something makes me think my new mate might have let his father snap his neck rather than fight against him. I look at Argon with new eyes, understanding a little more about what love is to him. Val returns with a huge med kit and begins working on him. He gives a pain inhibitor and something to slow the bleeding, and then he injects something that looks like foam into the deeper wounds. I'm horrified that he isn't going to make it, but I can't force myself to look away. When all the major stuff is attended to, Val backs off to give him some space to breathe.

After a few minutes the old man speaks. "They're all dead."

He doesn't ask it in the form of question, but Argon answers it anyways. "Yes, but you yet live. Focus on that for now."

Kryos gasps, moving to get comfortable. "He turned on us, got to the healers first and mauled their wings so they couldn't fly away. We thought to overpower him, but he was strong, fast and... relentless. No matter what we did, he just kept coming."

Since Argon doesn't ask who, I assume he knows about his lookalike.

"I managed to get away only because he didn't destroy my wing base completely. I tied myself to the tree to keep from drowning in the water when I passed out. I had no desire for you all to spend endless days searching for my body if I died."

Argon asks, "Why didn't he simply fly out to get at you?"

I supply the answer and ask one of my own. "He can't fly. Why didn't he simply go into the water?"

The older man sighs and clutches at his clothing trying to pull it together. I pull the two sides of his shirt together to help him retain some dignity as he answers my question.

"I am unsure. He may have run out of energy. He just stood on the bank staring at me. I remember thinking that he wanted to tell me something or wanted me to say something in particular. I was growing weaker by the moment and couldn't figure it out. The last thing I remember seeing before I passed out was him, still standing there, unmoving and covered in blood. He looked so much like you, Argon." His lips tremble, and my heart breaks for this older man.

My Argon asks tenderly, "What do you wish to say, my sire."

"Each time I spawned, I had nightmares that I had missed one of my eggs and that somewhere there was a tiny malnourished hatchling dying of neglect on our ship. In my dreams I wandered aimlessly through the ship searching for my lost spawn."

A new source of pain blooms in my chest. This must explain what was going on in the back of his mind when kept wanting to communicate with the creature. Alien or human, our brains all work against us at times.

Argon clutches his shoulder gently, giving him a shake. "You know better than that, my sire. We scan for our young, see the number we spawn, and such mistakes are an impossibility. With so many other warriors packed into tight quarters, someone would have seen or heard a hatchling crying out. It was just your subconscious worry about keeping us safe and far from our dame's notice."

"Our life before was so dangerous. We never knew from

one day to the next if we would survive. I'm sure what you are saying is true."

"Rest, now. We will take care of everything."

"No. I must warn you. Look for him with your eyes, for he doesn't make any kind of noise, even when he fights. He's fast and strong. Kill him from a distance if you can. Don't let him near your queen, Argon. Promise me this."

"I promise. Rest for now. All will be well."

Rruk speaks from behind us. He's out of breath and his wings are still out like they are when they've been flying. "He's nowhere to be found. I searched high and low."

Kryos relaxes back down to the ground. "We must find him before he makes it to the city or other settlements. The loss of life could be staggering."

"He will come back here. When does, we are ready for him."

"Come, my sire. We will get you to a healer."

"He killed four of them. Best just get me inside. I'll heal on my own. I won't risk another healer's life this day."

Argon's jaw locks but they do as he says. Val's already began cleaning up the massacre. The others join him while I make sure Kryos is comfortable. The older man's remaining injuries don't seem deep, so I close them with a dermal healing unit as he sips some healing tea he had me make from leaves in one of his many jars.

His hand closes over mine when I take his empty cup away. "Thank you, Queen Becca. You have been kind to me this day."

"You're more than welcome. I always wanted to be a nurse, so I enjoy caring for you this way."

He frowns. "I also meant thank you for selecting Argon as your mate. I know he can be a handful at times."

I give him a warm smile. "I really do think the world of

your son. He's good all the way down to his bones. He's been amazing to me. I couldn't ask for a better mate."

His smile is so genuine. Kryos is clearly pleased to hear positive feedback about his son. "Our people would say he has an honorable soul."

"We have a saying on Earth that the apple doesn't fall far from the tree. You're a good man and you did a fantastic job raising him."

"Thank you. Those four males are my entire world."

"Well, I'm eager to put this whole mess behind us and start making a family."

"That is my wish as well. In order for that to happen, we need to track this creature down and ensure it no longer poses a threat to our people."

"Do you have any idea what this creature was or why he was made to look like Argon?"

"No. I turned this over in my brain many times. Nothing about this situation makes any sense. We've never encountered a creature like this in all our known history."

"Maybe it's something native to this planet. On Earth we have stories of creatures who can take any form."

"Our people do not believe that is possible. The main piece I don't understand is how the creature could have been scanned and found to have my scion's exact DNA."

"Are the scanners loaded with DNA samples of all your people?"

His expression is confused, and he tries to sit all the way up. "What?"

I press him back down, but he doesn't go down because he's way too interested in our conversation. I give up and explain my train of thought.

"How would the scanner be able to make a DNA match if Argon's DNA sample weren't there to match it against?"

It takes him a minute to catch my drift but when he does, he nods. "You are a clever queen to suspect the scanner might have been tampered with. Go and ask Argon to retrieve the scanner. It should be near where he found the bodies of the healers."

"Are you going to be okay?"

He plucks his com device from the nightstand table and drops it into his lap. "I will message if I need anything."

"I don't feel comfortable leaving you alone after almost being killed."

When the older man lays back against his headboard, his wings squeeze out each side of his body. He sighs wearily. "If you only knew how many times this old warrior has been close to death, you would know how hard I am to kill."

I tug up the fur bed covering and scoot his fresh cup of tea closer before giving his hand a squeeze. "Rest, then. I'll be back to check on you real soon."

He closes his eyes almost immediately. I head out to discuss the scanner with Argon and look for some clues about what the hell is going on here. I feel like I'm being watched when I pass through the large, cavernous meeting room they all share. I'm certain that all the fresh violence I've witnessed is triggering my fear responses. I ignore the chill creeping up my spine and pick up my pace, practically running from the great room.

When the sun shines on my face, I feel as though I've survived a near miss, which is totally absurd. The bodies are gone, and the three brothers stand in a huddle talking. When I approach, I hear Val growl. "We will not abandon you when there is danger near."

Argon shoots back hotly, "This creature wants what's

mine. It will kill you all to get it. I alone have what it takes to defeat him."

I stroll up, cutting into their conversation. "Why don't we stop acting like an action hero and put our heads together to figure this situation out."

Argon holds out his hand and I move forward, slipping my hand into his. "What does it want?"

Argon's calm voice explains. "He was drawn by our mating last night. Remember, I told you how everyone with a nose for a great distance in every direction would know we were mated. What I did not tell you is that my mating scent is nauseatingly repugnant to other males, all save one. The one who thinks he is me. He is drawn to our mating scent and wishes to take my most perfect queen."

My knees get weak. Those innocent healers died because I drew the creature here. I don't know how I'm just minding my own business one minute and the cause of great evil in the world the next. My eyes close and Argon wraps a wing around me, tugging me close to his side. Why do I always check out mentally when there's a crisis?

"Where did he come from?"

"It does not matter, my queen. He is here."

I remember to tell him about the scanner. "Your father and I think he might have tampered with the scanner to make it read his DNA as yours."

"He is but the semblance of the warrior he pretends to be. Since semblance is not substance, I think the two of you could be right."

Tilting my head up to look at him, I ask, "Is it just me or are you getting to be a philosopher in your old age?"

"We understand his ways."

Val quips, "Who in the 'verse is we? Rruk and I don't understand any more than your fierce new mate." I'm with Rruk on this one. Argon is acting super strange and none of us know what the hell is going on. It makes sense that he's stressing out.

"You must take our sire and go far from this place. We will protect my queen. If you see the smoke billowing from my fireplace, then return on the morrow. If not, have our people gather their queens and leave this world. They must seek out another home world and never return. Do you understand?"

"So what is your queen, bait?"

Argon roars his fury at his brother's well-placed jibe. "My queen is my world. Our souls are now intertwined. Neither of us can survive without the other."

"Gods of chaos, you bred her like the queens of old? How did she even survive being staked?"

Val's totally overreacting, and I'm pretty certain that I don't like the stunning rebuke in his tone. This girl is just fine with our first intimate encounter, and they need to know not to second-guess him when it comes to his own queen. I turn on Val, coming off a tad more annoyed that I'm feeling. "Yes, he did, and his queen loved it. Now, can we move on from talking about our sex life?"

That comment wipes the disapproval right off his face. "I think one of us should stay behind to protect your queen in the unlikely event that you fall in battle."

"This bestial creature will target you first and you have no defenses against his thirst for blood."

"We are not walking off and leaving you here to face this beast alone. We always have a secondary line of defense. You know this is our way, Argon."

My huge warrior's expression closes down. "That was our way before encountering this particular adversary. Do you think I would insist upon this course of action if I weren't certain I could protect what's mine?"

"I think you're just about arrogant and defiant enough to believe you can win any battle."

"I have won every battle. Why do you think the creature chose my form instead of yours?"

My head snaps up. This is the first I've heard of him choosing his form. Argon almost makes him sound like a shifter.

"What if he sneaks up on you?"

I speak up. "He won't. We'll smell his stench a mile away."

Rruk chimes in, his tone evidencing the disgust we all feel at remembering the foul odor. "I know not how far away a mile is, Queen Becca, but I remember his vile scent well."

Argon speaks quietly. "It is the creature's version of a mating scent. It was triggered when he came to investigate our mating."

I cringe as I remember the shadow at the opening of our cave. It had to be the creature lurking around. I remember it crept away instead of flying away. That should have triggered a warning, a red flag that something wasn't right. It didn't, because I was caught in the thrall of Argon's mating scent. I shudder to think how things might have gone if Argon hadn't spotted it.

My shiny new mate points out something that should have been obvious to all of us. "It's mating scent will only get progressively stronger until it mates."

I shove back out from under his wing and glare up at Argon's impassive face. "The damn thing is not going to mate, not with me or anyone else." I'm furious at the thought of him getting his filthy bloody claws on a human woman. If a full-grown Draconian male can't fight him off, none of us would stand a chance.

Argon reaches for me again, his voice soothing and earnest. "Upon that we both agree. I will kill him before he so much as touches a strand of your beautiful auburn hair." I go willing to his side when he wraps up again in his wing. I love being close to him like this. It's getting so that I crave it.

Under normal circumstances I might even be impressed that he remembered the exact shade of my hair and wrapped his tongue around the alien word. Right now, I'm too stressed to be wowed by his dedication for me. Truth be told, I'm also weirded out by the strange headpiece he's wearing. It shimmers in a weird way that almost makes it seem like a million tiny insects squirming. Of course that's crazy, right?

Catching me staring up at his cool new helmet thingie, his lips curve up into a smile. "You are the perfect queen for me, my Becca. The gods have sent me a female who speaks her mind, misses nothing and is willing to punch a dragon warrior on the face for daring to touch me when I'm am down."

When he says the word down, he draws it out. I realize he's mimicking my slow southern drawl. Normally, I'd be mad if I thought someone was making fun of my accent. With Argon, I know it's because he's just fascinated by all the details. I impulsively jump onto my toes and kiss his chin. It's all I can reach, but it makes him smile.

He gazes into my eyes, and I swallow hard at the love and dedication I see reflected back at me. "Trust us to protect you, my queen."

I don't break eye contact. "You keep saying us even when you're sending the others away."

His lips curve up into a tiny smile. "Again, you miss nothing, my precious queen."

Okay, we're going round and round in a circle, and he's clearly not going to come clean about what's going on in front of his brothers. I back away and make a firm decision. "Take your father and get the hell out of here. Go before this monster gets a chance to attack him again."

"But..."

"But nothing, Val. Your father may be strong for his age, but we both know he won't survive another attack. Hell, it was a miracle he survived the first one. That creature ripped apart men half his age."

Argon joins me in trying to convince his brothers to leave. "Though our sire survived many challenges and his queen's claws, he is no longer the robust warrior he once was. We would all do well to remember that."

"He won't leave you. You know he won't."

"Tell him that Queen Willow has taken a turn for the worse and is begging to see him. He will not deny a queen, even though we are in some peril here."

Val frowns, balling his fists at his sides. "You would ask me to lie to my own sire?"

Without even blinking, Argon responds, "To save his life, yes."

Rruk speaks up, sounding annoyed. "I will speak to him. Lying about this suits me at the moment."

I don't have any idea what in the world he's talking about, but my nerves are on edge, so I say nothing as he walks off in the direction of his father's keep. Argon's hand comes out to land on Val's shoulder. "Go and gather a hover board and supplies. The medical station rendering care to Queen Willow is three hundred microns due south as the dragon flies. You should get there by nightfall if you leave right away."

"I don't like this. That creature is deadly and you're underestimating how vicious a male can be when the prize is mating a beautiful queen."

He glances down at me before answering. "I well know the worth of my own queen. Now, go before I become angry with your drooping wings."

Wing drooping must be a major insult of some sort, because his brother bares his teeth and growls before spinning on his heel and stalking off.

"I wonder why that abomination killed the healers. Do you think it was because he was afraid they would find out he was an imposter?"

Argon snorts a laugh. "Hardly. This being is afraid of nothing. I believe it simply wished to rid this mountain of all the other males to streamline killing me so it could fulfill its drive to mate quicker."

I can't keep the look of revulsion off my face. "I would never agree to mate with him."

"I am not certain it would give you a choice. The creature's mind is broken. It would mate you and sit on you until his young spawned."

My head is swimming with questions. Does Argon mean it would try to impregnate me or that he'd breed me until he activated his own reproductive system? Does he reproduce like the Draconian he's modeling himself after? The minute I think those thoughts, I want to burn the images they create from my mind. This entire situation is worlds away from anything I've had to deal with in my lifetime. All I want is for it to be over and our family to be safe. I need to stay focused and cover Argon's back.

I HEAR MY LOVELY QUEEN'S CONCERNS ABOUT THE scanner, and she is right to question this piece of information. I walk over and scoop it up from the ground. It looks unbroken, but I know this creature does not have my DNA. Therefore, I stoop and use a rock to crack it open.

Meanwhile, Becca has retrieved a laser pistol from the ground and shoved it into the empty case on her hip. I bought hers specially made for the small hands of a queen, and it's missing. I choose to worry about that later. When she kneels beside me, I hiss a warning. "Stay back, my queen."

Thankfully, she does shift back as I pry it open. The inside is contaminated with the thick dark waters of his lair. Long thin filaments as black as this creature's soul wind around and through the mechanics.

I hold out my hand and wait while Becca pulls out the laser pistol and places it against my palm. We both stand and take a few steps back. When we are out of range of possible flying shrapnel, I adjust the setting and burn the device until nothing remains but some twisted metal. Then I burn it some more for good measure.

Becca's hand lands on my arm. "Enough. I think you killed it."

Although she is trying to lighten the mood, I alone know that if even a small part of this creature remains, then it can replicate. When I am certain nothing is left, I do stop. By then even the many are screeching for me to stop. No one can hear them except me, but it does not matter. We will defeat this ancient evil, and unlike the many, I will destroy him rather than trap him in a deep dark cave he may one escape by chance. He will pay for the blood of my brethren he spilled this day.

A voice whispers through my mine. *His life has value. He has ascended.* I shove the voice away, for I care not about such things. My mind is made up, and I will not hear them when it comes to sparing his life.

Becca's hand slides into mine and she laces our fingers together. I know that I am acting strange when she holds out her other hand for the laser pistol. When I give it to her, she slides it into her case. If my queen had millions of voices speaking to her at once, she would act strangely as well. Soon it will be just the two of us, and she will know all that I have learned about our enemy. In exchange for their help battling this ancient being, I have promised the hive anonymity. That means that as long as they stay away, and the fragile peace I make this day is honored, none of my brethren will ever know of their existence.

I stand guard on the ledge while Becca makes food for us and starts a fire using her laser pistol on a low setting. As the sun sets, I feel the creature creeping near. He is eager and his stench is strong. My dragon is wide awake and rearing for battle. My scales have hardened and all I can think of is the many ways I might kill this being and ensure he never comes for my queen again.

A soft hand lands on my arm and Becca presses a drink into my hands. I start to refuse the wine because I must have a clear head, but then I smell the bean drink the humans love so much. I know it is a mild stimulant and will only make me more alert, so I sip the bitter brew. I do not know how human queens can be so enthusiastic about this bitter brew. It offends my palate.

She sits with leftover bits of food and some fruits I left for her enjoyment. Neither of us put our legs over the ledge out of concern of being snatched in case our enemy has crawled up once more. I eat only keep my strength up. My queen does nothing alluring to entice me into a mating frenzy, which is a blessing because all focus needs to be on remaining alert for the enemy.

"Do you want to tell me where this creature came from, and why he chose to look like you?"

I remove my head covering and shove it against the wall. The many will turn lose their bonds and crawl away to make ready for battle with the enemy. It is interesting to me that my queen is the only one of my clade who seemed to notice that the gold was an illusion created by the many so I could walk into Stone Mountain with them without anyone questioning me. My headdress held thousands and my armbands and the spear many thousands more. I have a virtual army at my back, all trained to neutralize our enemy, and no one realized anything was amiss but my Becca.

It is time to tell my mate all that I know. Since our bond is strong and pure, I will never leave her lacking for information, or speak words that are not true. She has elevated, and therefore in all ways we're equals. Protective I may be, but I will always give her the choice to make decisions for herself.

I start at the beginning. "We were wrong about this planet being uninhabited. There are ancient bioluminescent beings that live deep beneath the surface in gold glowing pools of water. They were once beings that appeared like we know aquatics, only they were much smaller, about the size of your hand. They were always water dwellers and communicated telepathically. Over the course of millions of years they evolved, shedding all but their brain stems, which over time shrank to tiny filaments that you can barely see."

"How do you know about them?" To her credit, my queen does not question the truth of my words.

"I stumbled upon them in the room you found me in today." Since the head covering is now gone, I take off the arm bands and lean them across the stone wall as well. "At first I thought it was all a dream, but I have since discovered it is not. They are very guarded with information about their numbers, but I suspect there are many. They claim to be prolific on most worlds but go unnoticed by other beings because they prefer isolation."

"Until one of them decides to go on a killing spree."

Glancing up to catch her eye, I can feel the many spreading out their protective net behind us. "You are more right than you know. There is but one being among them who spent thousands of years corrupting himself rather than reaching for enlightenment. Since the many do not kill their own, he was trapped in a single room below ground. The many visited him regularly, hoping to train him in enlightenment."

"Let me guess. He not only declined their generous offer, but he managed a little jailbreak."

"You are correct on both counts, my queen. Even though I have been to many alien worlds and seen many different species, I had a difficult time forcing myself to believe what I was seeing and hearing. They are very different from any species I have ever encountered."

"For some reason seeing is believing for me. I saw the sludge in that room move with my own eyes. Granted, I never thought it was a sentient being, but I already had it firmly in mind that it was something living. When you pulled Val back the sludge reached for his shoe."

"If the being had been successful, we might not be having this conversation. His presentation is not believable, because he used the information he obtained from the many who came to visit him to create a likeness of me. If he had made physical contact with my spawn-mate, the likeness might have been too perfect for anyone to have noticed a difference."

"Jesus, he might have been able to go to the city and lure one of the women to him."

"Since his soul is sick and twisted, I do not think she would have been willing or safe in its care."

"Neither do I."

"You believe my words?"

Nodding her face scrunches up into a delightfully confused expression. "Why wouldn't I?"

I gesture behind me and her mouth falls open when she turns to see the many. They are crawling along the indentations I carved into my wall. The design is a close approximation of what I saw in the cave. It is how they move about when not in water. It seems inefficient and strange to me, but I can hear their glee at having a new puzzle to solve. "I believe they enjoy the challenge of figuring out the design."

"My God, they're on your skin." Though her expression is shocked, there is none of the revulsion she demonstrates when we talk about the enemy. Her eyes are curious and interested. I hold out my arm so she can see the tiny wiggling filaments. There are only a few left, but each speaks, amplifying the voices of the many.

"They wish to speak to you. They don't hurt or feel very strange on my scales. Do you wish to accept their offer to speak?"

She stares at the filament on my arm, like I am offering her a curse disguised as a treat. "I promise you will not be harmed. Once the tactile link is established, you can sense their souls. They are good and mean us no harm. They are eager to get their brethren back before he harms anyone else."

"Oh, I have the opportunity to bond with an alien sentient, and all I have to do it wrangle my anxiety in check one more time."

"Facing down one's own fears is one of life's great challenges."

She shoots me a grin. "Your father has a wise saying for every occasion, and I believe you've spent a lifetime hearing them."

"I am guilty of stealing one of his favorite lessons for this occasion in my never-ending quest to impress you."

"You can consider that mission accomplished, babe." She raises her arm to mine and one of the tiny filaments inches towards her. If I thought for a moment there was a danger, I would never permit this link. The many are thrilled to be meeting a new life form. I feel their positive energy growing and the explosion of excitement when the link is made.

Becca smiles up at me. "They're saying hello." She laughs, holding her arm up for a better look. "They think having a name is strange. I'm being advised that we should recognize each other by our vibrations. They say every living being has a slightly different harmonic resonance, and we should learn to distinguish people that way." Her eyes find mine again. "They think names are primitive, as are mouths and anuses."

"I can hear every word the many are saying. Human brains must be very different from Draconian brains, because you're not annoyed that they're all taking at once."

"Humans talk over each other all the time. We get used to zeroing in on a particular voice in the crowd."

I love hearing their excitement that she has filaments. They're overjoyed until they realize the hair strands are not different beings all attached to a transportation unit on two legs. Joy fills my heart because I can almost see how they made that assumption.

Becca's gentle voice is conversing with another of the many already. "Oh no, there is a difference between a symbiont and a parasite. Parasites live off another being without providing a benefit to the host. Symbionts are two being joined together either permanently or temporarily for the good of both. We are enjoying a symbiotic relationship right now."

The many laugh at her explanation, believing that the link is not sufficient to establish a symbiotic relationship in and of itself. They insist that both beings must be relying upon each other for survival as well. I like being connected to my queen through the many. Her innate goodness and kindness shines through as well as her clever mind. We are both better for having had this strange experience.

The many all startle at once. I come immediately to my feet and pull Becca away from the cliff. Our enemy has arrived. One grime-covered hand grasps the cliff and then another. He hoists himself up, and when he comes into view, I realize he's even more repulsive than I imagined. He looks but little like me. His body is but a sad approximation of a proud warrior. His eyes are also strange. They move about the room, but they don't see. He senses us rather than seeing us visually. He knew of eyes when he made this form.

One gigantic hand slaps against the wall, touching the golden filaments that were only moments ago happily exploring the design I carved there. His voice pushes through the many. "I came for my queen." He's using the many to communicate with us. Of course he would do that. It's the only way unless we touch him. Even he's got to know that won't happen.

Intent on luring him into the trap, I step back. "Come, let us talk like reasonable beings."

"I have not survived an endless eternity to be lured into a trap by one such as you."

"Well, he's definitely not stupid."

His head snaps over to Becca and his body orients in her direction. "No female should mate an unworthy male. You are meant for a being such as me. Come with me now, and I will spare the life of this male you have mistakenly chosen. If not, I will remove him from existence."

"As tempting as that offer is, I'm afraid that I'm going to have to decline."

"Decline means no... refuse..."

"Yes. It means go away."

Becca's brazen words sting this being. We all feel it for there is no hiding one's emotions in the link. He does not understand why she would choose a lesser being. The moment he decides to kill me and teach my queen the advantage of mating with an ascended being, I shove her behind me and twirl the spear in my hands.

His unseeing body orients towards me, even though the

many cry out in unison for him to stop. They know we are now locked in a life-and-death struggle, and one of us will die.

My Becca is still in the link and scratching around for information on how to destroy our enemy before he can kill me. Little do they know, I already sourced this information. It happened when I slept deep in the cave. When one sleeps in the link, their mind is free to dive into the many rather than waiting to see who speaks. I learned many things they do not wish me to know.

The many suddenly know my thoughts, as does my enemy. I curse this mind link and break through all their wails and move forward. The entire wall of filaments fling themselves past me, unfurling into a golden net. They cover their evil brother and shove him backwards off the cliff.

I follow and land just in time to see them forcing him through the ground. It is, perhaps, the most repulsive thing I have ever seen. It looks like they are forcing a being through a sieve, taking only the bits that make up the entity himself. They leave behind a lump of dead tissue and bones, all bloody and cut into pieces the size of my claw. Since one of the many still clings to me, I hear his horrified screams as they pull him from his fabricated body. I am still at a loss as to how he made this strange body. He didn't will it into existence after all.

The many say nothing on this mystery and it is the one piece of information I was not able to get while I slept. The many are sad beyond measure. I feel them pulling him down into the depths of the planet, where they heave him into an ancient tomb. It's dark and cold, and once they crash the lid down, there is no hope of escape. I can hear his despair, and I know he still does not understand the wrongness of his actions.

Becca has scrambled down the sheer rock face by herself. The look on her face is a mixture of grief, anger and relief that it is over. "It doesn't matter if he understands. He won't hurt anyone ever again." I am surprised that she speaks of the question that was only in my mind, but I remember we are still connected by the many wiggling on our skin.

I move closer to her and further away from the gory mess on the ground. "This much is true, but I find the lack of vengeance an unsatisfying victory."

Our filaments drop to the ground with a final warning from the many to honor our agreement to keep their existence secret. I hate that I have agreed to this. However, they are harmless beings and I fear my brethren would destroy them to keep this planet we love so much.

Even now the many long only to return to the depths of their cool pools of water where they will swim, converse together and sleep. Their life is a leisurely one. One of their days is so slow a year passes among our people. They truly experience time differently once they are together in their natural habitat. I doubt we will ever see them again, so it seems a small price to pay to rid ourselves of one evil being.

They believe those of us above the ground waste our lives in endless and unnecessary toil. I am not certain if I disagree, but I do know that I would rather be here with my queen than swimming in their underground pools.

I must admit his words haunt me. *I have not survived an endless eternity to be lured into a trap.* He didn't see his brethren's physical attack coming at all. His shock jolted through us like a bolt of lightning. If he had not killed four of our healers, I might feel some pity over his being locked away for all eternity. He'll likely dry out and fade away before many years are up.

Argon and fell into bed exhausted last night with no sign that any of the many had stayed behind. Today the sun has just crested over the horizon and we're snuggling in bed.

Argon snorts a laugh at our morning banter. "Do not lie to your own mate. You like everything to do with me, including my keep. You also like my warmth, my mating scent, my fine carvings, and most of all, my cock."

Turning over on my side, I use my hands for a pillow and smile at him. "I never said I didn't like all that. What I said was, we should have a separate room for sleeping."

"Dragons do not like extra rooms. We like one large space with enough room for our mates and our hoard."

I make up my mind to be devious. "Well, I noticed you don't like other people seeing your hoard items."

He growls, "That is why we do not visit each other's space. Dragons are territorial about their possessions and their mates."

"You mentioned that. What if we had a huge second room for the bed and your hoard? No one would ever see your queen naked nor would they set eyes on your precious hoard." That gets his attention. Hiding his naked queen and his gold and gemstones must hold some appeal because he doesn't immediately say no.

"I did not like our enemy sneaking up on us during our breeding. Perhaps there is some merit to this idea of a secondary chamber in our keep."

"Yes, it is a good idea. Then we wouldn't have to worry about males flying by our cave and seeing us lying around talking when we should be mating."

He immediately reaches for me. "You think we should be mating right now?"

I scramble closer. "To be honest, all this talk about an extra room for our bed has gotten me a little excited. I love having extra space."

He frowns. "The extra space is for a bed *and* our hoard."

"Yep, I don't know how I forgot about the hoard. Your hoard items are really important. I should have said, 'and extra space for your hoard and our bed' to show how much more important the gold and gemstone is, right?"

His expression is warm and admiring but his tone a little disgruntled. "I can tell by your tone that you did not mate me for my glorious hoard. You do not seem to value hoard items the way my kind does."

I reach out and give him a nice long stroke. "No, I certainly didn't marry you for your treasure. I married you for you cock."

"Among my people, queens control their males by being in the dominant position during breeding."

I snort a laugh of my own. "There ain't no position in the 'verse that will enable me to control you, big guy. You and your dragon are way too incorrigible."

My words remind him that he's prone to follow the beat of his own drummer, and he likes that. His face lights up with lust and he jerks his chin. "Come ride your sex-starved dragon warrior. He's been waiting all morning to feel your silken sheath clench around his cock."

"When you talk dirty, you really go for the gusto, don't you babe? Lie back and grab the headboard above your head. I'm going to lay you out for my pleasure the way you did me."

Staring at me like I just grew a second head, he slowly reaches for the headboard. It's really just a relief carved into the stone wall, but my guy's all about pretending with me this morning. When I begin to scoot down his body, he lifts his head to look down. "What are you doing, my queen?"

"I'm rewarding my mate for agreeing to build a new hoard room." See what I did there? I left out the part about the bed and stressed the hoard part, cause he's my most precious possession and I want to keep him happy.

When I wrap one hand around his already-hard cock, his eyelids flutter. I know he's thinking about how much he enjoyed me jerking him off in the tub. I've got a sexy surprise for him though. Flipping my hair over to the other side of my head so he can see what I'm doing, I lick over the end of his cock with my tongue. He jerks in my hand so hard, I almost lose my grip.

I glace up to see what kind of effect I'm having. I'm about to tease him, but I see literal smoke coming out of his mouth. Not taking my eyes off him, I lick around the head in a gigantic circle, because he is pretty ginormous. There is a sexy growl, another curl of smoke and he breathes it in through his nose. I can't be certain, but it seems like some kind of calming technique he's using to keep from losing his shit.

Sensing it's now-or-never time, I concentrate on giving the best blowjob of my entire life. I suck the first inch or so into my mouth and swirl my tongue around the tip. He tastes smoky, but I can't place the exact flavor. I like it though, so I keep right on licking all through his squirming and sexy growls. When he speaks his voice is so low that it almost sounds animalistic. "Ride me now, my queen."

I don't want to stop though, so I kind of ignore him. That's a really big mistake, because his tail snakes around my throat, and he tugs me gently up. It's such a dominant thing to do that I'm practically gushing.

I throw one leg over his hip as the tail slips down my back. Bracing myself on his abs with both hands I and lift slightly. He seems totally fine with that because I'm doing what he wants. It's really fortunate for both of us that what he wants is what I want as well. If not for that, I'd make him suffer my erotic torment until he came.

"I see your devious mind working out the details of your revenge for bending you to my will."

Intent upon beating him at his own game, I sink down on his cock while verbally teasing him. "I was just thinking that if you hadn't insisted upon this position, I could have sucked you until you were ready, and then let you cover my breasts in your seed. You could have rubbed it in and made me wear it all day so everyone would know I'm your queen. Just your queen and no one else's."

That really gets to my ultra-possessive dragon. I can tell because his eyes drop to my breasts and he growls, "I wish it, my queen."

"Too bad, we're already doing this now." I lean forward, rise up, and drop back down. His head falls back, and he groans my name.

"Becca, what you do to me." By this point, I'm pretty far

into my zone. I swivel my hips, chasing perhaps the biggest orgasm of my life and when it hits, I feel like my head is going to explode.

Argon doesn't come through. He's holding out like a champ, and I'm pretty sure I know why. He rolls us and slams into me so hard that I squeal with delight. Something about a nice hard fuck with a sexy dragon outranks every other experience out there. The moment I come a second time, he pulls out and shoots onto my chest. God, I must be a total freak, because I love watching him come on me.

He's in that position I love so much. Looming over me, he's all huge muscles, sexy fangs and wings. If someone asked me to describe my fantasy man, it would totally be Argon. He's hot, sexy, and dominant as hell.

He doesn't even stop to catch his breath before he's rubbing his spunk into my skin. He even stops to play along the way, running the blunt side of one claw around my nipple. I realize at some point he's making cute designs in his own spunk, like he's decorating me with it.

I can't help but laugh, partially because he's so focused on it, and partially because I'm ticklish. "Let's get a shower and something to eat."

His dark eyes lift to mine. He looks a tiny bit embarrassed and a lot stubborn. "You know that is not going to happen, my sweet and generous queen."

"Your woman is starving, probably because of all the energy we've burned this morning. Are you honestly going to deny her food?"

"You may have food, but no shower."

My mouth falls open, because I was only joking about wearing his scent. He's still really turned on, so I know he's not joking at all.

"Fine. I do get to wear actual clothing, right?"

"Yes, but I get to pick your gown."

When he sees that I don't think this is funny anymore, he clarifies. "I will pick your gown for today. If you do not care for my possessive nature, do not provoke it while we are mating, my competitive queen."

Well hell, he's got me on that one. All my anger evaporates. "Pick me something pretty with matching jewels."

His pleased expression is back, and it's a good look for him. He's really happy that I'm wearing the huge gemstone necklaces he bought me. Truth be told, I've never owned anything even approaching nice before I came here, so I'm allowing him to indulge me in a few luxury items.

I think I may be able to change his mind about the shower though. "You're a really handsome man."

"Warrior."

"You're a handsome warrior then."

"I know. Few have as many battle scars as your mate does."

I sit up and he backs away to make room for me. "You know, I'm glad you don't have self-esteem problems and all this referring to yourself in the third person is a little pompous. You know that, right?"

"I use your title in place of your name all the time and have yet to hear an objection."

I grin at my big warrior. The man's got a brilliant mind. He does refer to me as my queen all the time.

Pulling back the blanket, I slip my feet over the side of the bed and turn to look at him over my shoulder. "Am I ever going to win a disagreement with you?"

"If I were docile like the males from the city, you would not wish to be my queen."

"You are absolutely right about that, handsome. Want to

know something about why you're so much more interesting than they are?"

He nods, as if he's not sure he wants to hear.

"After spending weeks around warriors who agree with everything you say, it feels a lot like you're dating yourself. You, on the other hand, are your own person. I like that you speak your mind, and you don't always follow the rules. That makes you unpredictable, and miles more interesting that the others.

"You're still not getting a shower this morning."

I bust out laughing. "Leave it to you to think my sweet compliments are an attempt to get something from you."

He moves closer and curls around me, much like I expect a dragon would if he shifted into one. "You speak the truth then? You like me better than the males in the city?"

I nod. "Yep, that what I just said."

"You like me better than the other males of my clade as well."

I'm not sure where that question came from but he's acting so serious that I answer it without teasing. "Yes. I definitely prefer you over every male I've ever met."

"I prefer you out of all the females I've ever seen as well."

I know he phrased it that way because he's seen more females than he's met.

"You and I are forever, right?"

"Yes sir, we are. I don't plan to ever leave you. We're going to have lots of little ones and a long and happy life."

"This is more than I ever hoped for before."

"Me too. On Earth there are few males and many females. I never would have found a husband there, much less one as amazing as you. Coming here was the best decision I've ever made."

"It was. We are perfect for each other, are we not?"

I nod my agreement. The sunlight catches the highlights in my hair and Argon, runs a strand between two of his claws.

I reach out and trace his brow ridge with my fingers. "I think we are perfect each other. I can't imagine being with anyone else but you. You're my everything that matters."

"I am not. Your queen friend matters to you."

I shrug. "She does, but she's got her own mate to worry over now, right?"

He dips his head before mumbling, "Yes. Narcis may be young but he will stop at nothing to ensure she is happy and well cared for."

"Well that's real nice. I'll always want to visit with her regularly but you're where I want to put the majority of my time and effort moving forward."

"Not to change me, but to show love for me."

He's gone from phrasing things as a question to phrasing them as a statement. That tells me he's finally getting it.

I give him a long lingering kiss on the lips. "I wouldn't change a single thing about you." I grin up at him before slipping in a little teasing. "Not that I think you'd be very easy to change. You're pretty set in your ways. I mean some people might call you stubborn, but I'd never use that word.

His expression lightens. "I like that you make the human jests with me. It is nice and makes me feel bonded to you."

"But let me guess, I still don't get to shower this morning, right?"

"Come shower with me."

"Really?"

"Yes. I will mark you with my scent again after."

Gee, that's real sweet of you, babe."

"I know. The gods have given me a precious mate. I am obligated to treat her well."

I want to howl with laughter at how far off base he is with that statement, but I don't, because I don't want to hurt his feelings. He might be all claws, fangs and hard scales on the outside but he's soft and easily hurt on the inside. I glance down and apologize for something I know hurt his feelings when we first got together.

"I want you to know that I lied to you about something, Argon."

His claw comes up under my chin and he lifts my face to look into my eyes. "Tell me, my queen."

"That day I told you to get out because I didn't want to smell your mating scent. I lied about that. The truth is I was scared and wasn't totally sure you hadn't eaten my friend. When you asked me to sit on your lap some small part of me really wanted to take you up on that, but I was too angry and worried about my friend to let go of my fear."

He runs the blunt side of his claw down my cheek to my neck before whispering in my ear. "I knew you weren't being honest about that because I could scent your arousal, much like I can scent it right now."

"You're not playing fair when you use that sexy voice."

Pulling me back down into the bed, he coos, "Don't you know that dragons never play fair? We play to win."

When his mouth covers mine, I find that I am aroused and needy again. Once again, Argon's got me all figured out. What's more, he's giving me what I need almost before I realize I need it. I revel in the feel of his scales sliding against my skin and his hot mouth on my skin. This is what I've always wanted and needed. I'll never let him go nor will I ever take him for granted.

ARGON

I am evil on the inside, and there is nothing to be done for it. I've allowed my delectable little queen to shower, dried her off, and marked her with my seed all over again. She thinks I'm strange, but once she suggested this, I could not refrain from taking her up on her suggestion. Even now my spawn-mates wrinkle their noses at the scent.

Her loud little friend queen has no clue what is going on or that we're properly mated. Queen Willow just got back, and they are even now hugging and laughing together. So much has happened over the last few months, but as long as I am strong for her, my queen seems unaffected. Pride surges in my chest that I have a queen who relies upon me so heavily.

"Stop looking so smug, my scion. Luring a queen is not nearly as difficult as keeping her interested and safe."

"Do not tell me of my own queen. She has dedicated herself to me, as I have done for her."

"Now that you have killed for her, I don't doubt you're feeling possessive. Don't mistake your feelings for hers. That would be a foolhardy mistake."

"She wishes to mark me so all will know I belong to her."

My sire's head comes up hard and fast. "No human queens have requested this. It is the old ways. I am not happy to see you branded again. I wished for better than that for my young."

"You should know that human queens have a long history of decorating their bodies with colorful ink. My queen has requested a design that is unique to represent our joining. She wishes for us both to wear the mark in honor of our union."

"What is a union?"

"It is the word humans use for mating. It is when two beings unite themselves into a family unit of two and their young for life. It is called a marriage, union, pair bonding..."

My father interrupts, "Yes. I have heard of these other terms. Now I have a new one to add to my vocabulary." He drifts into a thoughtful silence. "This is much different from being branded as property, is it not?"

"It is different. I do not feel any lack of respect, particularly since she has left creating the design to me."

His wings droop for just a moment, but he recovers quickly. "You are honored by your queen. Have you given some thought about the design?"

"I recently began researching our database and some of the designs are like captured images. They can be complex or simple. "I was thinking of something like a small locket with our images."

"That sounds lovely."

"Are you not going to ask about the creature we destroyed?"

My sire's hand moves to his stomach where the creature wounded him the deepest. "We saw what was left of him. I must admit that I cannot imagine how you killed him that he ended up in small chunks. I hope you did not emotionally scar your queen by doing such in front of her."

"We faced the creature together. My queen is stronger than she appears."

"Of that I have no doubt. I heard about her attacking your spawn-mate for striking you when you were unconscious."

"He's lucky her hand didn't find her laser pistol at her waist. He might have suffered a more permanent injury."

My sire stares out over the flat stone pavement we laid in front of our common area at the two human queens. "Humans seem so slight and delighted with even the smallest gestures of goodwill. Yet their minds are quick, and when their anger fires it seems they fear no one."

"Human queens are like nothing we have ever known. Their capacity for love and devotion is rare. They even grow attached to those of us with ancient blood. My dragon would kill for her, as would I."

"I worry that there may be others like the creature that came for her. Who knows how many are lurking in the wild or when they might become bold enough to approach again."

"I can assure you there are no more such as the one we killed."

"Where did it come from?"

"I believe some things are better left unknown."

"It is not in my nature to let things like this go, especially when we now have precious queens to protect."

Intent upon getting his mind off the creature, I spring my good news. "You should think more on your scion and less upon their queens."

His stunned expression lets me know he has no idea what I'm talking about.

I preen a bit. "You will soon be offering me all manner of compliments."

He shakes his head, "There is something very wrong with you, Argon. I know not what it is, but it affects your thinking at times."

My hand goes to my side, and I tug down the leather covering my lower half just enough for him to see the swollen egg sack.

"You will be pleased that you are first to know. Not even my queen is aware, for I wished you to perform a medical scan to make certain all is well."

"Congratulations, my scion. You have done well in securing a beautiful and dedicated queen and are now breeding for her. I am very proud to call you my young."

"Did I not just say you would be showering me with compliments?"

"Nothing can spoil my good mood, not even your arrogant ways. Come, let us see if all is well."

We slip past the others and into the small alcove we use as a medical station. Since we are so far from the city, we've gathered a marginal amount of equipment to do us. It is mostly all handheld equipment, but I can foresee that changing once we begin bearing for our queens. My sire is far too contentious to risk his grand young's health because of old or faulty equipment.

A gruff voice sounds off from the doorway. It is my long-lost spawn-mate, Narcis. "Tell me you are not with young already?"

I preen all over again because this is one of the proudest moments of my life. "Of course I am. Are you not with young already?"

He growls, and I realize that even though he has spent many weeks with his queen, she was either too ill to mate, has rejected him after all or he has still not come into his hormones. I think it is the latter because of the petulant look on his face and the fact that she returned with him.

My chest aches for him, but I try to stop being an unmitigated ass for one moment. "Correct me if I am wrong, spawn-mate but none of the males from the city your age are yet mated. Yet, here you stand with a beautiful mate with fire-colored hair."

His expression brightens. "This much is true."

"Many of the fully functional adult males in the city have no mate. There are five other mountain clades scattered through this region and none of them have queens. Am I right once more?"

He finally grins at me. "What you say is true. We do our clade proud by bonding with two beautiful queens. We are the only clade in the mountain with a breeding male as well."

I laugh with pure joy in my heart. "I must say it is far better to be selected by a queen before your hormones come in than wait for endless years afterwards for a queen. You are in the best possible position. Surely holding, touching and tasting your queen is more than enough pleasure for the time being."

Finally, my spawn-mate is preening as well. "Tell us how many, my sire. I wish to shout from the treetops that our clade will soon have young."

My sire stands, staring down at the screen on the scanner. "There is one."

I make a grab for the scanner. "Only one? That can't be right."

Suddenly my youngest brother is the one giving

support. "One is better than none, spawn-mate. It is one more than all the other clades in these mountains have."

"I wish for two or three. One is not a fitting offering for such a devoted queen."

Narcis takes a step closer. "I came from a spawning of one and grew up to lure a queen before I even came into my own hormones. Do not disparage spawnings of one."

I set aside my disappointment. "What you say is very true, spawn-mate. I will be forever grateful for what the gods have given me instead of always wishing for more."

He reaches out to grab my arm and begins yanking me to the door. "Come and let us make plans to reveal this good news to your queen."

"I will tell her, and she will be thrilled."

Narcis shakes his head. "This is important news. You cannot just say it with words. We must devise a cunning way to communicate it that is both fun and surprising. My queen explained all about spawning reveal parties. Humans have them all the time."

I'm dumbfounded that we must host a party to alert our queens that we are spawning. It seems almost too absurd to be true. However, he pulls up the information in the human database and it appears he is correct.

"We need something that communicates spawning in a visual way."

"Perhaps I can gift her with a jewel shaped like an egg."

"That's a really good idea but think bigger and more intense."

I look at my spawn-mate with new eyes. "How about a larger gemstone shaped like an egg?"

"You are not very good at thinking abstractly."

"It does not matter. I am good at breeding. My queen will be thrilled with that alone."

"You still need to make telling her a grand statement."

Throwing both hands up, palms out, I say with frustration, "Why don't I just carve a huge stone boulder into an egg and decorate the front of Stone Mountain with it?"

He stares at me and I glare right back. At some point we both smile. This is an outstanding, over the top, and very permanent way to announce that our breeding has been successful. It is a perfect homage to my queen, and a standing monument to mark that I am the first in my clan to produce young. Oh, there is so much I like about this idea that my spawn-mate has forced upon me.

We break company as he goes to search out the perfect boulder and I head to my keep to scratch out a plan. We have laser drones to do the carving, but I must come up with the initial design and programming for the drones. I wish to make the egg as detailed as possible so she cannot mistake it for anything other than our young.

I draw my charcoal down a clean white page and begin lightly roughing in the grid that will serve as the three-dimensional parameters. Unlike the eggs of most species, ours start out small and grow along with our young in a flexible shell that hardens over the course of several lunars.

They are usually dark, but the color of the egg reflects the little spawn inside. Mine will be battle green like me. There is often a subtle texture or even a scale pattern but that is not always the case. If there is a nub at the top, the child is a female. If the egg has no nub it will be male. Since my kind only produce males, I am already certain he will be male.

Little spawn are the greatest gift a male can offer to his queen. Though my queen is deserving of more than one lone spawn, perhaps if we start with just one, she can better understand how quickly our young grow and how rambunctious they can be.

I bend over to my desk and sketch until my drawing is an intricate work of art. Next, I grab my handheld com device and scan the image into a three-dimensional modeling program.

WE WISH TO KNOW MORE ABOUT YOUR HOME WORLD. The voice echoes through my head even as the single golden tendril wiggles on my skin.

I've been banished to the back of the great cavern in the heart of Stone Mountain. I know Argon is working on a special gift for me. I think it might be the matching tattoos, but I can't imagine why that would have me hiding out in one of the back rooms like this. It's a good thing I brought my beading and a friend to keep me company.

"Well, our planet is really far from here. It takes almost a year to travel there at top speed. I came here because my planet is dying."

Planets should not die.

"Humans took a really long time to grow up and we did a lot of damage to our planet. It might take millions of years for our atmosphere to recover. In the meanwhile, we can't breathe the air, and nothing grows."

What about the many? Do they not protect your planet and keep it balanced?

"I don't think we have the many on Earth."

This is why your planet suffers.

"I wish we'd had your people there to help us. We would have been a lot better off. Right now a lot of innocent people are suffering for the bad choices of the people who came before us."

You didn't ascend.

"Nope. We sure didn't. I'm not sure any of us knew anything about ascending."

We can teach. It takes millions of solar cycles to evolve.

"How are all of you doing since you had to lock away your poor decision maker?"

Many of us miss him. His resonance was unique, and his mental abilities were superior.

"I don't doubt it. That's probably why he escaped. He was too smart for his own good."

This we know.

"I'm sorry you can't be with your friend anymore."

We wish he had not killed.

"Well, we're probably like the beasts we kill for food to the many. You're ascended and we probably seem pretty primitive by comparison."

Some of the many resent losing a unique mind because he took the lives of four primitives who ate other primitives every day of their lives. It is hard for us to understand your ways.

"Heck, when you phrase it that way, I have a hard time understanding our ways as well."

We like your harmonic resonance.

"Aww, that's a sweet thing to say. I like all of you as well."

Except the one with a unique mind?

"Well, I didn't hate him or anything. I just needed him

to stop and he wouldn't. If there has been another way, I would have jumped on it."

We are pleased that you see his life as worthy.

"I only wish he felt the same way about my people. He didn't see the ones he killed as having value. They were healers who dedicated their lives to keep us healthy. We valued them highly."

We agree. That is the reason he was exiled.

"I wish things could have ended differently."

As do we. I must return to the many. Being away too long damages us.

"Well, we wouldn't want that. I would love more conversation if and when the many would like to visit."

We will be back. Now we must go. Your mate comes.

The little filament scampers away. I have no idea how it found me or how it's going to find its way home. Since they've been living on this planet for millions of years I'm pretty sure they know their way around.

The door swings open and Argon comes strolling in. He's smiling and that's enough to make me happy. It's only been a few days since the attack, but we're slowly piecing our lives back together. I feel safer than I ever did. Argon's been less snarky and more doting than I ever thought possible. I'm of two minds about that.

"Hey there, handsome. How are you doing?"

He stops dead in his tracks. "I am doing very well." Thumping his chest with one clawed fist, he states, "I am strong and capable. Why would I not be well?"

"Calm down, I was just asking because of your mystery project. I don't know what you've been up to and I worry about you."

Holding out his hand, he grins. "I will show you what has been taking most of my time."

I hop up and we walk out hand in hand. When we step out into the sunlight, something huge is casting a shadow over the entire courtyard. When I turn around, I discover it is a huge stone sculpture. Of course it's stone. Everything in and around Stone Mountain is made of some form of stone. His huge round, egg-shaped statue is no different. Using my hand to shade my eyes, I give it the once-over. I realize it's not only egg-shaped; it's a strange alien egg of some sort.

Why would Argon have carved me a huge egg? My mind is still grasping for the answer when I look over at Argon. He's so flipping excited that it finally hits me like a ton of bricks. We're going to have a hatchling, and my new alien husband has a ginormous ego, so naturally he carved me this nice giant monument to his breeding abilities.

My hands fly to my face to cover the squeal of delight. "We're going to have a hatchling?"

He nods, almost too emotional to respond. I gesture for him to show me. He turns slightly and slips the top of his pants down on one side. Sure enough, there is a gentle swell in the exact spot the three-dimensional training program said there was a sack for carrying eggs. I already know Draconian males are super sensitive about how many young they're able to carry at one time. Since Argon is huge, I'm assuming one at a time.

"Can I touch?"

"Yes. It will feel slightly warmer than the rest of my scales."

I place the palm of my hand over the small raised area and surprised by what I feel. "Your scales here shifted into battle armor." Before he can explain, the reason pops into my mind. "It's to protect this area while the egg forms, right?"

"Yes. In about twenty sun rises it will be ready to incubate."

Argon is really patient with me while I fawn over his little alien egg sack. I know that sounds gross, but it's not. The slightly warm hand-sized bulge is hardly noticeable until you're really looking for it. This little surprise will teach me to pay more attention to my man. I lean over, press a kiss over the area and stand. "This is the best surprise ever. Now, come here. Your face needs my kisses on it."

He bends down and I slip my arms around his neck. He lifts me, keeping me on the side that's not currently carrying our young. Giving him a million kisses is just the prelude to the longest and sexiest kiss we've ever shared.

The recent attack put my life into sharp perspective. You never really know what the future holds. Argon and I could have been seriously injured or even killed. I'm not willing to wait any longer to start living the life I've always dreamed of. This child represents our shared future together, and I can't wait to hold him in my arms. Meanwhile, I will just have to make do with keeping Argon in my arms.

"What a difference five months makes! I went from thinking that you might have killed or eaten my best friend, to falling in love with you, to getting mated, and now we're about to have our first hatching break out of his shell."

We've moved our incubator into the great room. Even now every member of my clade is preparing for our first hatchling party. Warriors are coming from all over these mountains to see our son come bursting from his shell.

We have been closely monitoring him all day and adjusting the temperature to ensure he is not overheated. When he emerges from the shell, his already doting mother can finally hold him in her small human hands.

When I look down at my beautiful human mate, I cannot imagine a more agreeable life. She wears a likeness of my face inked onto the front of her chest. It is small, dainty, and set into the likeness of an ornate locket. The dark colors are lovely against her pale skin, and best of all, it signals to everyone with eyes that she is my mate. Of course, I wear a more masculine image of an ax cleaving my chest with her face reflected in the metal. We are both well pleased with our matching marks. It is all anyone who has seen them wishes to talk about. We hope that having this hatchling will shift the conversation to our child, because we tire of talking about our marks.

My queen's amused voice draws me from my internal thoughts. "This is the point in the conversation where you talk about how wonderful our life is, and how happy you are that we found each other." This is my mate's not-so-gentle reminder that I am not holding up my half of the conversation.

I quickly let her know my feelings on this subject. "Our life is a genuine pleasure. We are both agreed."

Then I switch up the conversation to something she is not expecting just because I'm feeling evil in this moment. "I have been thinking of getting my cock tattooed with an image of your naked form. What do you think?"

She frowns at my ingenious idea. Running her hands over her baby bump, she sighs. "You only want to do that because I am pregnant, and my baby bump would show well across that raised oval bump on your cock."

I pretend to be shocked by her words. "I would never consider preserving your lush pregnant form on my cock for all eternity for such devious and lewd reasons."

Smiling at my pathetic acting ability, she says, "Liar. I know you better than you know yourself, Argon."

My hands come out to reverently cup her belly. "You are not carrying just any young. My precious little queen grows inside your womb. Such an auspicious achievement should be immortalized in ink. What better canvas than my glorious cock?"

"Yeah, we're not having this conversation on our son's hatching day."

"That is fine, my queen. We will talk of this at a later

date."

Her bland reply is less than satisfying. "Umm, no we won't."

Picking up a sweet from the table, I bring it to her lips. "Have a delicious morsel so our little queen might be as sweet as her beautiful mother."

"You know, you're really on a roll today. I'm not sure how to handle you when you're like this."

Holding out my hand, I use my most seductive tone. "Come, my queen. Spend a few moments in my arms before the room fills with guests. You are the rock that grounds me when my life is changing, and I know not where to turn."

She eyes me suspiciously, no doubt wondering why I am being so outlandish today. I do not fully understand it myself. I just know that I am overly excited by the pending birth of my queen and seeing my little spawn for the first time today.

She allows me to snuggle up with her in one of the large padded chairs our queens insisted upon cramming in our great room. I must admit they are comfortable enough for both us to rest comfortably.

My queen has piled her auburn locks high on her head in an elegant arrangement. It is one she reserves for special occasions. I love this style because it exposes the pale column of her throat for my mouth to explore. I wish she would tell me that my face needs her kisses on it, but I think she is too preoccupied with meeting our son for the first time today.

I smooth my hands over her stomach even as I drop small kisses along the side of her neck. She makes a tiny sound of pleasure and that along with having my arms full of her softness makes my cock twitch.

"Don't get yourself worked up. It's going to be a long hatching party, and we are not leaving early."

"Umm, if that's what you think, then you do not know your mate very well."

"We still haven't chosen a name."

Inhaling her wonderful scent, I murmur, "Names are important. We must choose carefully."

"What are some common names for little warriors among your people?"

"You do not want to know."

She turns to glance at me over her shoulder, and I can tell by her expression she does wish to know. I sigh that am forced to tell my sweet queen yet another story of our life in the time before out liberation. "The most common name is Draq."

Her expression shifts to one of anger. "I've already heard this story. One of the human women had to rename her mate because Draq is the generic name given to males when their Draconian mothers find nothing unique or special about them."

"There were tens of thousands in the before times. Fear not, our queens found many clever ways to communicate our low status. Kryos is an old-fashioned word for 'zero' in our tongue. My sire was named this because his dame determined he had zero qualities to recommend him."

"That's horrible. Your father is a wonderful man. He should not have been named disrespectfully."

"Agreed. We do not speak of it in our clade. Many warrior were named Neglit, Gong, Mamuli, Kurang. The names mean Ugly, Be Gone, Trivial, and Deficient. My spawn-mates and I were envied by our peers because our dame did not care enough to visit or name us so that responsibility fell to my sire. Argos means First Light. Valixon means Valor. Rruk means Luck. And Narcis means Handsome."

Finally her scowl turns to a smile. "We should follow your father's fine example." She toys with the fastener on my fancy shirt, the one we bought especially for this occasion. "What do you think about the name Noble?"

She wishes to name our son the word for a being of high status or rank. My chest fills with pride because this is a perfect name for a little warrior. "I approve. Any male would wear such a namesake proudly. I will ensure he knows that such an honor comes with much responsibility."

When she smiles up at me, her face is radiant. "Thanks. I didn't know if that one would meet with your approval or not. I think it has a nice ring to it."

"I have been thinking of names for our tiny queen, and one name calls to me like no other. In fact, I must admit that I have been referring to her by this name for the last two lunars in my own head."

"Tell me. I'm excited to hear what you have had rolling around in your head."

"I think of her as Precious."

My queen's hand goes to her mouth like it is prone to do when she is faced with a shock or surprise. "I love it, babe. I say we go for it."

"You permitted me to select the name of our queen?"

She leans over and kisses me on the nose. "Yes, and you did a wonderful job."

This is much different from the life I knew before coming to this sector of space. Here my queen loves our male and female spawn equally, no matter which of us sheltered them in our bodies. My people are truly leading our best possible life on this new home world. I for one will never take our life here for granted, for my queen has taught me that the price of freedom is constant vigilance.

My sweet queen makes herself comfortable on my chest and we speak of all our plans for the future. She toys with the tiny, finely crafted gemstone egg pendant I created to mark our first son's hatching.

Soon the room begins to fill with the many visitors who have come to witness our son break free of his shell. We are forced to forgo each other's company to greet our visitors. My sire ensures the ale flows freely, and I introduce my pregnant queen to every male in the room. Do I wish to rip their eyes from their heads because they stare at my lovely mate while she is heavy with our little queen? Of course I do. I am a primitive and possessive male after all. Will I ever do such a thing? Most likely not since my queen would disown me. I have learned that human queens take pleasure in the company of others, for they are very social creatures.

As the evening proceeds, we stay close to the incubation unit housing our little warrior. My Becca's eyes are fixed upon our egg and she rarely looks away.

Just as the sun sets, my queen nudges me with her elbow. "Your son is causing a ruckus."

I look over to find our egg is vibrating. I motion to my father and we all gather around to see how long it takes him to break free. My Becca is annoyed that some of the males make bets. I am amused and feel sorry for those who bet it will take him long, for I know my hatchling is strong and confident.

"Oh, I'm so excited. He's really moving around in there."

"Yes, my queen. I remember breaking from my shell. I spent a little too much time looking for a tool to crack..."

She elbows me again. "Cut it out. I have it on good authority that the gods don't like liars, babe."

I rub my tender scales where my lovely has elbowed me twice, not because it hurts but because if she thinks it does, I will get extra kisses later. "Tall tales are meant to be told at hatching parties, my queen."

"Quiet. He's already cracked the shell. Look at that!"

I cannot blame her for being excited. I am as well. We watch as the crack gets longer and wider until he pecks a big chip out with his tiny clawed fist.

Someone yells from the crowd, "It is a good punch. He's going to be a mighty warrior."

Others cheer. Maybe the warriors in the city have hatching parties that are tamer, but those of us in the mountains, we are a rowdy bunch. A new hatchling is a one of our life's most important events because historically so few us were bred. My queen seems surprised and bemused by our enthusing.

With each additional thud against the interior of the shell there is more thunderous celebration than before. Even my normally sedate sire is on his fifth ale and pounding the table in a vain attempt to help my hatchling establish a rhythm of battering his way out of the thick shell.

My own spawn-mates are staggering around the room, refilling glasses with happy faces. I have never seen them so delighted to be reduced to barkeeps.

I spy Narcis' loud queen climbing onto our huge stone dining table. Since she has no young filling her belly, she is far more quick and agile than my own queen. She puts two fingers in her mouth. I quickly cover my queen's ears because I know what is coming next. A loud shrill noise comes from her mouth, and she yells out to my queen. "What did you name him?"

Since the room has gone quiet, my queen barely has to raise her voice. "We named him Noble."

Whispers break out around the room, growing louder by the moment, and suddenly the room is bursting with conversation again. The revelry is unparalleled because this is the first hatching party among the mountain region.

Queen Willow begins chanting our hatchling's name over and over as she punches the air with her fist. For once, I approve of her loud behavior. Everyone joins in the chant and within moments my little hatchling has burst from the shell with a mighty roar. Truth be told, it was more of a squeak. However, to my mind it is an indication that he is not to be discounted and will make his displeasure with the world known as he grows up.

I lift my own queen onto the table, as her friend slips away. My sire already has the incubation unit open and is reaching me my newly hatched little warrior. I cradle him in the crook of my arm and climb onto the table for the showing.

My queen takes him to her chest and tucks him into the bodice of her gown. The warriors all make sounds of approval that she warms him against her soft skin. Our hatchling roots around against her kind, familiarizing himself with her scent. His wings flutter. I have no doubt he's eager to stretch them after being in the confines of the shell for the last few months.

Tucking my wings behind me, I lift my chin and wrap my arm around my queen and young. "I wish to thank the human queens for coming to settle on our world, and for selecting brutal primitive warriors like ourselves as mates."

I pause while the males lift their ale and sound off their agreement. Most of these males were our crew mates on the risky voyage to this new sector of space. We have fought together and bled together. I know them well and respect them all.

"Thanks to the human queens, we now have a chance to make a future for ourselves. I am surely the least likely male to lure a queen, yet here she is." When all eyes turn on her, I don't mind because she wears my mark, stands by my side and holds my young. I announce proudly, "My Becca is soon to gift me with a little queen to shelter under my wing."

There are some more cheers, jeers that she is too good for me and offers to join our clade. I ignore their playful banter and go on to make my final point.

"If one such as me can lure a lovely fire-haired queen, then surely all of you can secure a queen as well." Lifting my little hatchling from my queen's arms, I hold him for all to see. His plump body, tiny wings and thrashing tail remind us of what is most important in life. "This is why we all fought so hard to survive the rule of Draconian queens, so that we might continue our lines. Let us fill these mountains with our young, so their ties of love and matings might bind us together and make us strong."

The cheer that goes up is almost enough to shake the very foundations of our mountain home. My son's head lifts, and he flaps his wings as if to fly away from the racket we make. Although I wish to hold onto him until he is old enough to establish a keep of his own, I hand him back to his eager mother and accept my first cup of strong ale for the night.

My sire's eyes are practically glowing with happiness from across the room. I lift my glass and when he does as well, we drink in honor of the newest member of our clade.

———

TRUE TO MY WORD, I steal my queen and little warrior away early. My clade will continue to drink into the wee hours of the morning, but my pregnant queen needs rest. She barely lets me hold my own hatchling. She's too enthralled with running her fingers over his soft scales, smiling at him and whispering sweet things to him. I believe she has forgotten she has a mate. Still, there is a grin on my face that won't go away, and I'm just jealous that haven't received a fair turn.

I pad around setting up one of my housing units in the wall to keep him temperature-controlled and safe from crawling or flying away. When all is ready, we place him in the unit and close the door. He flops down onto his stomach and stretches his wings. Not surprisingly, he's asleep before we get the unit closed.

"We can't just leave him here. What if he needs something?"

I wrap my wings around Becca and begin tugging her back. "Draconian young are not like human babies. Ours come out of the shell scavenging for food, sharpening their claws and trying to fly. The unit has to close in order to contain his active form."

"It seems cold and uncaring."

I snort a laugh of disbelief. "You are the softest queen I have ever met. A hatchling will make noise the moment he wishes for something that he cannot procure on his own. See the little boxes built into the back of the unit? They are stocked with foods that will sharpen his teeth, water, manipulative items designed to amuse a newly hatched little warrior. When he squeaks, we will run to see what he needs. Unlike human newborns who need constant attention, hatchlings need space."

"I read all that in the database. I just can't get my head and my heart on the same page."

"Come we will watch him while we rest."

We pad over to our bed and remove most of our clothing in order to sleep comfortably. When we lie down, she turns towards our hatchling and I become the big spoon. Becca demonstrated the concept of human spooning to me, demonstrating with real spoons. We attempted to switch it around one time, but I am much too large, and my wings got in the way. Also my tail was far too eager to explore what was lying against it. So, now I am only allowed to be the big spoon. This suits me better anyway.

Just when we settle down, our little warrior makes a sound. I am greatly surprised since he was sleeping just a moment ago. Before I can even sit up, Becca is out of the bed and back with him in her arms.

"He's wide awake."

I roll over onto my back and spread my wings so she can lie on her back beside me and be comfortable. Noble crawls around all over both of us and is much more active than I remember a Draconian hatchling being. He makes little cooing noises, and I know he's likely going to be a handful.

As I watch my queen tenderly interacting with our hatchling, it hits me that we are not going to be able to raise our little one like my sire raised his scion. He is too active and already demanding attention and free rein of our home. His human mother also has her own ideas about how little ones should be treated.

When he falls asleep sprawled out face first over her stomach after chattering to his soon-to-be sibling, I give up. He looks far too adorable and my queen is far too happy being hands-on with him. I turn on my side and close my eyes. Tomorrow is another day, and I suspect we will need our rest if we are to chase after him all the hours of the day. Still, my grin won't go away, and I fear it will be stuck there for all time.

REBECCA

THERE ARE DEFINITELY PROS AND CONS TO GIVING birth to a Draconian child. Pros are six-month pregnancies and smaller but somehow more robust babies. Cons are an entire clan of overprotective males fussing over you day and night. Most women would think males anticipating your every need might be really cool. For the first couple of months it was heart-meltingly sweet. Along about the third month it began to get on my last ever-loving nerve.

Since Argon won't tolerate anyone in our personal space, I'm now holing up in one of the back rooms with a huge fireplace and a huge bed. Argon thinks it's safer for me to be down here where his whole clade can protect me in case their one and only enemy on this planet comes back or the many decide to renege on their agreement. He'd probably be pretty upset if he knew I was still talking to them. I don't tell him because, well . . . they seem nice, and what he doesn't know won't hurt him... or them.

The thing is, a girl needs more than a fireplace and bed to get by in life, especially when she's just about to give birth. Sure, Willow visits several times a day, and I've got my jewelry-making equipment, but the last few days I've been feeling antsy and anxious. I wish I could get out and walk in the wilderness or at least help out around the place. Besides feeling a bit jittery, I've mostly been bored out of my mind. An image of a juggling bear on a unicycle pops into my mind unbidden.

Your male should be more entertaining. My visitor wanted to touch my belly, so I agreed. The many are curious creatures and seem fascinated by human breeding. I answer because this one is really sweet.

"Yeah, I know. Unfortunately, for that to happen he'd have to calm down for just a second and stop being so paranoid."

Our males perform water aquatics and turn bright colors for our amusement.

I watch my new friend slink across my naked baby bump, but I can barely feel her against my stomach. She's not cold or slimy like I imagine worms to be.

I can hear the others agreeing through her neural link. They send images of groups of them performing colorful and perfectly choreographed water dances. I send them back a mental image of humans performing our version of the same. Though the many excel at this type of dance, and I think they'd see our efforts as comical, they're excited that humans have something similar.

We are pleased to discover yet another quality we have in common with humans.

"Yeah, that's kind of cool."

Your child wishes to be born.

"Well, I certainly hope so. She can't stay in there forever. Human babies are born when their time is up, not necessarily when they want to."

She comes now, human queen. The many celebrate

by moving quickly in their pools and talking excitedly over each other. Slipping quickly off my belly, my tiny friend scampers away. She's a sneaky one, always popping up when I least expect her and making a clean getaway before anyone shows up. How does she do that?

I run my hands over my belly, wondering if they could be onto something. Maybe that's why I've been so jittery. I sit up and scoot to the edge of the bed, reaching for my chime when a sharp, drawing pain makes me freeze. Within seconds it's over. The many were right! It is time.

I hit the button several times and deep chimes echo off the walls throughout the cave system. I take a deep breath and steel myself for what is to come. Giving birth for the first time is anxiety provoking no matter how prepared one is.

I hear their boots pounding on the stone floors before I see them. Argon is panicked. I can tell because his wings are clicked out about thirty degrees and his tail is wrapped around his own leg.

His father is carrying our little one. He's only about a month old and still sleeps most of the time. He has a nickname already—Scargon, after his father. I came up with the name because Argon is so proud of all his scars. Unbelievingly, he considers it a name of honor. Scargon looks cute tucked into the crook of his grandfather's arm, dozing. His little tail is limp and lifeless, swaying gently as they move across the large room. His delicate wings aren't big enough to lift his body weight, but I'm told he'll soon grow into them.

Argon is on one knee inside of moments. "Are you well, my queen?"

"It's time. I had a contraction."

"Call in the healers." Argon bellows at the top of his lungs.

I reach out to smooth my hand down his cheek. "Calm down. It'll be a while yet. Remember the contractions start out far apart..." Another contraction hits and I'm shocked that it came so soon.

I am wrapped in Argon's arms before the pain eases. His wing is draped loosely around my back as if he knows now is not the time to wrap me tightly to his side. When I look into his eyes, I expect to see joy at the birth of his long-awaited little queen but his expression is tense and worried.

I lean onto his chest and murmur, "I'll be fine. Women give birth all the time."

"Not my woman." His expression turns almost pained and he glances away. "You are my world. I have no wish to see you in such pain."

"I know, babe. Just hang tough and this will all be over soon."

I no sooner get the words out than several healers arrive with a portable scanning platform. Argon lifts me onto it as they pull out all the bells and whistles to make it fully functional. Argon hovers, like he's wont to do, and they kind of work around him.

I'm not certain if these particular healers are familiar with human births because they remove all my clothing and clear sides slide up the sides of the platform. The next thing I know, the unit is filling with a clear blue liquid that smells vaguely antiseptic. Argon elbows them out of the way with a growl and begins running a soft sponge-like square over my body. The liquid is warm, so other than being stark naked in front of everyone, it's not uncomfortable. These healers seem a little germ phobic. I guess they aren't taking any chances when it comes to human birth, especially one involving a female child because they are so rare among the Draconian.

The contractions come hard and fast as he bathes me. The moment the liquid drains, he dries me off with a thick cloth. "All will be well, my queen. I will not leave your side."

He's a real sweetie, but at this point I'm just having one contraction after another and I want it to be over with. I never expected the contractions to run so deep or feel like everything in my torso was tightening and drawing down at the same time. This can't possibly be normal.

When I finally get a sterile covering, the softness and warmth is such a relief. I know Argon would normally be freaking out that other men are looking at me and seeing what he calls my queenly treasures, but he's so freaked out and worried about me and the baby medically, that's clearly the furthest thing from his mind.

He's so much less snippy with the healers that they are giving each other strange looks. I find the way he keeps smoothing his hand down my arm and holding my hand relaxing. I know they've given me something, because the contractions are stronger but feel less painful. When I look up into Argon's now only somewhat distressed face, I realize whatever the blue liquid was, it was spiked with something to take the edge off. Bless those crafty healers getting a twofer that way.

The more-bearable contractions continue getting closer together until the healers start telling me to push. I just can't imagine where I'll get the strength. I'm exhausted and sweaty, but I know that I've got to do this thing. That's when my dragon warrior leans over, and all I see are muscles the size of mountains, wings, horns, and sexy fangs. "You will push now, my queen. You are strong, and our little queen needs you to follow the healer's directions."

When he takes both my hands in his, I gather all my remaining strength and push. Though it seems impossible, they ask me to do it all over again.

I'm such a mess that I barely realize that I've successfully birthed our daughter. Argon turns to look behind him, and when he turns around there is shock and awe stamped all over his face.

"Is she okay? Tell me what you saw."

"The most inglorious battlefield cannot compare, my queen."

What the hell does that even mean? Luckily, I don't have long to work myself up into a frenzy, because I hear a startled scream. A short, high, piercing one that communicates that she's angry with this new world. Then something really unexpected happens. Another scream rends the air. This one is from Scargon, who's now clawing to get out of his grandfather's arms.

Poor thing probably thinks I'm dying or something. I reach for him and Argon lowers him onto my chest, keeping his hand locked around his lower half. My little one is really in a tizzy, and at some point I realize it's not me he's concerned about. It's his newborn sister. Something about her continuing cries is really setting him off.

When the healers finally deliver her into my arms, he moves closer and licks at her face. She stops crying, and he snuggles right up beside her and makes himself at home. Something about seeing them take comfort from each other reminds of the siblings I've lost and how close we were. When I tear up, Argon loses it.

He hisses his displeasure instead of his normal roar, cause he's not about to disrupt the little ones now that they're quiet. "Finish clearing the battlefield. My queen needs to rest."

Okay, so we all know exactly what he means but I don't know how I feel about my afterbirth being likened to a battlefield. I'm not going to complain, because I'm grateful my mate is present and participating. He leans back over me and blocks out the overhead lighting. Suddenly, we become a family of four. In my mind the healers fall away. His family hovering at the door fades into the background. There is Argon, our little ones, and me.

I feel something metallic slip into my core and warmth spreads throughout my pelvic region. I remember something about their healing technology from all the information they sent me to study. They're shrinking my uterus and healing me one hundred percent right away. I'll be able to stand up and walk without pain. I thank every Draconian god for advanced technology. They give me little hydration pellets with some kind of strange pink liquid and they not only quench my almost unbearable thirst, but they give me an energy boost as well.

Time seems to crawl slowly by. Argon cleans the sweat from every square inch of my skin with the sponge thingie from before, only now he's dipping it in the calming solution. He murmurs supportive things to me and cleans his little daughter, not stepping back until it's time to pick me up and return me to my bed. My bold warrior doesn't do that though. He picks us up, allows his father to bundle a heavy blanket around us and takes me up to our keep. I keep the little one safe and cuddled in the blanket against the cold.

He lowers us carefully down to the bed and pulls up extra blankets, including the one made of fur. There's already a fire burning in the fireplace. He takes a moment to stoke it and bank it down with huge logs before returning to our side. He voice-prompts the shield over the entrance to our keep and peels off his clothing down to his unders. The thin grey underpants come down to his mid-calf. Since he didn't bother with them before, I assume they're a new introduction because we've got little ones.

I pull back the side of the blanket, and he grabs a hydration pack and slides into the bed. We carefully move the little ones to his chest, and I watch his eyes dancing with pleasure. My mate practically has little hearts in his eyes, and I can't help but feel so lucky.

"You did well, my queen. Our little female is perfect." Holding up one of her tiny five-fingered hands, he murmurs quietly, "She has your hands."

I run a finger over her wing base and glance up to look into his eyes. "She has your wings."

He snorts a laugh. "Those are not the wings of a warrior."

He's right, of course. They're smaller than Noble's wings and much more delicate. She'll be lucky to one day fly under her own power with those frail wings. I don't say that though. I focus on the positive. "She's got nice horn buds."

"Yes, but no tail. This will be a problem. All the males will wish to mate her."

I'm surprised by that announcement. Catching the expression on my face, he explains. "Tailless females are considered exotic. I do not wish my tiny queen to be thought of that way."

"Aww, it's sweet that you're protective of her, but she's going to end up taking a mate one day. You might just as well get your head around that right now and save yourself some angst."

"I will call forth only the best and bravest warriors for her to choose from. Our little queen deserves only the finest mate."

"Yeah, maybe we could let her choose her own mate. She might like a healer, rather than a warrior."

Snorting another laugh, he deadpans back, "No queen would choose a healer over a true warrior." Lifting his chin as if challenging me to disagree, he states. "Healers do not have even have battle scars."

I frown at him, wondering if he realizes how far off base he is. When his lips turn up at the corners slightly, I know he joking with me.

"There you go again, jesting with your queen. You should be ashamed of yourself."

Leaning over to give me a quick kiss, he whispers, "Yet I am not. I wish to stay on this sleeping platform for many days, jesting with my queen and holding my young."

I grin at him, thinking about how fantastic that sounds. It's not remotely feasible, but a nice fantasy nonetheless.

His next words catch me off guard. "Never did I expect to be gifted with a queen, much less one who finds it in her heart to care for me. Next to his lovely mother, our son was the most beautiful sight I had ever seen. Most of my brethren will never have a little queen to call their own. She is more precious to my heart than even my hoard."

"For a dragon warrior, that is a high compliment indeed."

"Do not worry. I immortalized the occasion. Your magnificent form during your time of carrying our young was far too lovely to let it slip by unnoticed."

"You got the tattoo we decided you weren't getting, didn't you?"

The smirk on his face tells me he did just that, but I'm

in no mood to see it. Instead of incriminating himself by admitting it, he looks deeply into my eyes and talks himself right out of trouble with me. "I am forever in your debt for seeing the worth in one such as me. You have given me your heart and two young to call my own. I agree with my brother's loud queen about one thing. I am living my best life with you at my side."

There's no stopping me from tearing up. My hormones are probably still raging and he's being sweeter than normal. I lift our daughter off his chest when she starts rooting around and bring her to my breast. Argon's eyes light up to see his daughter trying to nurse for the first time. His hand comes out to smooth down her wings. "She will grow strong with the sustenance you provide."

I'm still emotional and blink back tears as she finally latches on properly. "I love you, and I'm really glad I took a chance on jumping on that Draconian freighter. Thanks to you, I'm also living my best life."

His lips come to my forehead and he kisses me, lingering to smell my hair. Everything about this situation calls to me as a woman. For once all my anxiety has disappeared, and all I can think of is how wonderful our life will be.

Ready for more sexy Draconian adventures? Read Alien Defender's Chosen Bride (Draconian Warriors Book 8) now!

Akes – Draconian god of hunting, war and violence. He is the consort to Entares, the benevolent goddess worshiped by Draconian males.

Antar – Right (Lutar is left.)

Avada – Small carrot like vegetable that is seasoned and wrapped in a dry leaf.

Challenge –Draconian queens settle disagreements and property disputes by challenging one another in single combat. It is usually a battle to the death.

Clade – Group of Draconians who are descended from a common set of genetic code.

Dark Star – Another term from black hole.

Doma – Type of Draconian flatbread.

Dracon Two – The name the second wave of Draconian warriors nicknamed their new home world. Dracon Two's real name is Onello. It is located in Naxis space. The planet was originally named by Queen Cassandra after a Greek god. It was unofficially renamed Dracon Two because the name their new queen chose is very near the word for feces in the Draconian tongue.

Draconian - Species created by mixing dragon DNA with humanoid DNA. There are many family lines with unique strengths and weaknesses.

Entares – Draconian goddess of beauty, peace and joy. The males worship her as she represents their desire for females to show kindness and respect to them for their many sacrifices, rather than the harsh treatment they normally receive.

Entaza – Dish eaten with the living larva still wiggling in the dish. Common food in Exion space.

Exion – Vast Sector of space encompassing the Draconian home world. Exion is ruled by a race of ruthless females bent on conquest and power.

Hatching – Draconian method of reproduction by which warriors conceive and carry eggs.

Hatchling – Noun: Child. Hatching is a verb: Act of creating young by a male Draconian. Males hatch many times during their lifetimes.

Hatch Mate – Refers to only the children hatched during the same cycle of breeding.

Laser Pistol –A weapon used in battles and self-defense which uses power packs to fire short laser bursts.

Lunar – Equivalent of a complete phase of the primary moon traveling around Dracon One. This is a standard unit of measurement used by many space faring species, even when not on their home planets.

Lutar - Left. (Antar is Right)

Maradox – Queen Ravonda's ship, which was boarded and taken by Queen Cassandra and Mathadar.

Moltan – Malevolent aliens who attack and destroy other vessels.

Naxis – Vast sector of space encompassing five galaxies, including the Milky Way.

Parsec – Unit of distance. Used mostly in determining distance in space.

Parthenogenesis – Draconians males undergo parthenogenesis when exposed to a female's pheromones. It results them incubating eggs in their bodies which are released into specially designed incubators.

Phase Grenade – Device that sticks to the hull of a ship and disables their weapons.

Raspian – The second mother ship and one Hope and Larok use for the voyage to Onello.

Revidian – The word used by Draconians to denote a warrior performing oral sex on a queen.

Scion – A word used for offspring, no matter the age.

Solar Revolution – Equivalent of a complete revolution of Dracon One around its sun. This is a standard unit of measurement used by many space faring species, even when not on their home planets.

Spawn-Mate – Draconian equivalent of brother or sister.

Strovian – Race of warriors who are at peace with the Draconians in the Naxis sector.

The Obsidian – The name of their ship.

Takadon – The Draconian word for a male who is chosen to be the queen's primary breeder. He is to stay at her side constantly and is her protector.

Taladar – Species who initiated a trade agreement with Earth to exchange much-needed food and other supplies for human brides.

Tankea – Draconian word meaning love between a parent and child or between siblings.

Tricon – Unit of thickness.

Unders – Anything worn under one's uniform or regular clothing.

Utaka Larva – Pupa stage of growth for a tiny colorful flying creatures the Draconians keep for pets.

Vithacan – Symbionts that attach themselves to other creatures and survive off their emotional energy. Soul suckers is a disrespectful term for their race.

Zelerians – Race of squid like creatures with few humanoid features.

Juno Wells grew up on Florida's Space Coast, watching the shuttles take off from Cape Canaveral. When she hit college, her childhood fantasies about space travel turned highly romantic. Now her mind reels with space adventures of fantastic alien lords in distant galaxies, and the earth women they love.

Wells' stories explore the complex, sensual relationships between inhabitants of different star systems. There are always happy endings just as there is always a new world to explore.

Her work is exclusive to Amazon, so read as much as you like with Kindle Unlimited.